"I'm Matt Gramling. New in town."

Karla took his hand, releasing it as quickly as she could. The same spark that she remembered from their interview seemed to flow up her arm. That same sexy smile had her knees feeling decidedly wobbly, and that same intensity he brought to bear at work showed as he gazed down at her.

"I'm, uh, Karla. Do you know me?" she asked warily.

He tilted his head a moment as if listening more intently. "You look familiar...."

NINE TO FIVE

From boardroom...to bride and groom!

**A secret romance, a forbidden affair,
a thrilling attraction?**

Working side by side, nine to five—and beyond....
No matter how hard these couples try
to keep their relationships strictly professional,
romance is definitely on the agenda!

But will a date in the office diary
lead to an appointment at the altar?

Find out in this exciting new miniseries
from Harlequin Romance®.

Look out for
The Boss's Daughter (#3711)
by Leigh Michaels
on-sale August 2002

HIS SECRETARY'S SECRET

Barbara McMahon

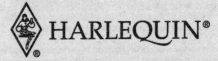

TORONTO • NEW YORK • LONDON
AMSTERDAM • PARIS • SYDNEY • HAMBURG
STOCKHOLM • ATHENS • TOKYO • MILAN • MADRID
PRAGUE • WARSAW • BUDAPEST • AUCKLAND

ISBN 0-373-03698-1

HIS SECRETARY'S SECRET

First North American Publication 2002.

PROLOGUE

KARLA JONES sipped her water and pretended to study the menu. In actuality, she was eavesdropping on the conversation at the adjacent table. The trendy Vancouver waterfront restaurant was crowded. It was almost one o'clock—the lunch hour just ending. Here and there checks were being paid, people gathering their things in preparation to return to work.

Recognizing several women at the adjacent table as secretaries from the company her friend, Pat, worked for, she idly listened to their chatter.

Karla liked to take her lunch break later than most, to avoid crowded restaurants. Already more and more tables were becoming vacant. In just a few minutes the women seated at the table behind her would disperse. The general din of noise would soften and her lunch would be more relaxed for it.

But now, she found their conversation fascinating.

"...heard he'd be closing the entire company down within the month," one woman said in hushed tones.

"That's dumb, why buy it if he plans to shut it down?"

"I heard he's going to move it lock, stock, and barrel to Toronto. And hire a whole new staff there."

"I heard Miss Evans gave notice today."

That comment startled everyone into silence. Karla almost jerked around to question the statement. Miss

Evans? Wasn't she the president's executive assistant? Karla was sure Pat had mentioned her more than once over the years.

Karla was surprised at the news. Almost as surprised as she'd been last week when she'd been told her own boss, vice president David Daniels of McCormick & Associates, was retiring almost immediately. She herself might be out of a job if Mr. Daniels's replacement wanted a different secretary.

"Well, it wasn't because Mr. 25-50 is into age discrimination—except in a reverse way," someone behind her said.

They all laughed.

"Don't worry, Suzanne, you're only twenty-four, still in the running."

Everyone laughed again as they divvied up the check and gathered their things. In only a few moments, they'd passed Karla's table without glancing her way, still talking about the mysterious new CEO of their company.

She watched them leave, wondering if any of the rumors had any basis in fact. Especially the one about Miss Evans. If she were leaving, was this fate's way of letting her know about a new job opportunity just when she needed it?

"Hi, sorry I'm late. The call of nature, you know." Pat Carns eased herself into the chair opposite Karla two minutes later.

"Can you fit?" Karla asked teasingly. Her friend was eight months pregnant and seemed enormous to Karla.

"Very funny. Just wait, one of these days you'll get married and the next thing you know—you'll be as big as a whale yourself. What looks good?"

"Everything on the menu. I'm having salmon."

"That sounds perfect, I'll have it, too."

Once their orders had been placed, Karla studied her friend speculatively. "Without breaching any confidences, can you tell me if your Miss Evans is really leaving?"

Pat blinked. "How in the world did you know that? She just gave notice this morning." Pat worked in the Human Resources Department of Kinsinger Electronics. The two friends had met in secretarial school eight years ago, hit it off instantly and remained close ever since. They rarely discussed business when they got together, however. Karla's confidential secretarial position dealt with a trade firm for Pacific Rim commerce while Pat's dealt with employee relations of an electronic manufacturing company. Neither were given to breaching confidences.

"It can't be a very big secret. There were several secretaries from your company discussing it before you came in. I overheard—as could almost anyone in the place," she said, glancing around. The tables were close together. Many were empty now, but earlier the place had been crowded.

"Someone should speak to them about the concept of confidentiality." Pat shrugged. "If it isn't a secret anymore, it won't hurt to tell you she gave notice this morning. She said she couldn't work for anyone else since Mr. Moore wasn't going to remain in charge."

"Was it she didn't want to work without Mr. Moore—or not work for the new guy?"

"I couldn't say, but I'm sure she's heard the rumors about Matthew Gramling—he's said to be a real slave driver. And the company is faltering, there's no denying that. Miss Evans was approaching retirement age anyway. Maybe she just didn't want to have to deal with a dynamic hotshot after her years with Mr. Moore.''

"Not deal with Mr. 25-50?''

Pat grinned. "Heard that part, too, huh?''

"I heard it. I don't get it.''

"Well,'' Pat leaned closer—or as close as her protruding stomach would allow—and motioned Karla closer. "The rumor mill says he never dates women over twenty-five and never hires women to work directly for him if they are under fifty.''

"Why?'' Karla asked.

"Apparently women over twenty-five are worried about their biological clock and put a lot of pressure on a man. I take it our new CEO is definitely not in the market for a wife.''

"Sounds like he has a monumental ego problem to me. Does he think every woman he dates wants to marry him? And the under fifty part?''

"Worried he'll train someone and she'll get married, have kids and leave him in the lurch.'' Pat sat back and laughed as she patted her stomach. "And he's probably right, look at me.''

Karla smiled, but said nothing, her thoughts whirling. Her boss was leaving and her own situation tenuous. The secretarial slot for the CEO at another company was opening up. A perfect opportunity for her to move ahead.

"I want Miss Evans's job,'' she said.

"Didn't you hear what I said, the new CEO doesn't hire pretty, young women to work for him. He'd take one look at you and show you the door, certain you'd be on your way to the altar in no time.''

"But I'm not. And have no plans to be anytime soon, either,'' Karla said firmly. ''I've worked hard for eight years. Getting married anytime soon just doesn't fit into my plans.''

"Yeah, yeah, yeah. I've heard that. Once the right guy comes along, you'll change your mind.''

"Even so, it wouldn't necessarily mean I'd want to quit my job. I like working.''

"Whomever they promote to Mr. Daniels's place will love to have you,'' Pat said loyally.

"Unless they bring their current secretary with them.''

"Then you'll find something else. But not Miss Evans's job.''

"Am I not qualified for it?'' Karla asked bluntly.

"Of course you are. You have all the training and skills of a highly sought-after executive assistant. But you're forgetting Mr. 25-50's rule. No one under fifty for him.''

The waiter brought their salads and placed them on the table, effectively interrupting their discussion.

Karla thanked him, and began to eat, changing the subject.

But she wasn't finished with the idea. She'd find a way. This opportunity seemed too perfect to pass up. She'd been working since she was twenty, first for an ambitious manager, then a seasoned vice president. The next logical step was to a CEO's office.

And the perfect opportunity had just presented itself.

She'd just have to figure out a way to circumvent Matthew Gramling's convoluted notion of what constituted the proper age of an executive assistant!

CHAPTER ONE

KARLA pushed the button to the twentieth floor. She looked neither right nor left, but stared at the burnished-bronze elevator doors as the car swooshed quietly upward. She recognized one or two others from Kinsinger Electronics on the elevator, but, afraid they might realize who she was, she refused to look at them directly.

Granted the few times she'd stopped by to pick up Pat probably hadn't made an impression on anyone, still, she took no chances.

Butterflies danced in her stomach. She resisted the urge to check her hair again. Touching the natural-looking wig had the tendency of calling attention to it. Trying a small smile, she could feel the stage makeup pulling against her cheeks. Polly assured her the coating looked natural—though it wrinkled once she smiled or frowned—adding at least twenty years to her appearance. Or so she hoped.

Active in little theater productions, her friend Polly had a huge case of makeup aids. She'd been delighted to help Karla age herself—making her promise to call her as soon as the interview was over to let her know how the disguise worked.

The tinted glasses perched on her nose were annoying, but necessary. As were the staid, plain, classical designs of her business suit and low-heeled shoes. The wig was hot and made her scalp itch. It would all be worth it, however, if she got the job.

By the time she reached the twentieth floor, Karla was alone in the elevator. Stepping out into the quiet lobby, she instantly noticed the thick carpeting, the subdued lights, and the soft music. Quite a difference from the offices in which she'd been working. Of course, McCormick & Associates had been feeling the crunch of the Pacific Rim trade and was much more cost-conscious than Kinsinger appeared to be. She had enjoyed working for the firm, and would miss Mr. Daniels. But she had to look to her future.

There was no central set of desks housing staff on this floor. No hustle and bustle of a hectic work area. In fact, as she headed toward the office of the CEO, she wondered if she were alone on the floor. Surely someone else was around.

The quiet murmur behind one door assured her the floor wasn't deserted.

Entering the office with Miss Evans's name still on the door, she saw a huge wooden desk in solitary splendor—neat as a pin. Miss Evans had departed last Friday, according to Pat.

The door beyond stood ajar. Karla took a deep breath and stepped forward. Show time. Could she pull it off? Rapping sharply on the door, she reviewed all her plans. She thought she'd covered everything. The interview would show if she had or not.

"Come in." The deep voice touched her senses, sending a shivering spark of awareness skidding across her skin.

She pushed open the door and stepped inside the large,

corner office. Two walls consisted of tall windows, providing a beautiful panoramic view of the harbor with North Vancouver in the distance.

Spectacular as the view was, it was the man who rose when she entered that caught her eye.

Karla's heart skipped a beat and settled down to a fast pace. No wonder Matt Gramling had an uncomplimentary view of women throwing themselves at him. In his case, it was probably justified.

He was heart-stoppingly gorgeous. Tall with broad shoulders, he looked as if he should be advertising race cars or sleek yachts. His dark hair was styled perfectly for the boardroom, but for one startling moment Karla wanted to muss it up, run her fingers through it to see what it felt like. See it tossed by the wind, burnished by the sun.

She caught her breath. Was she losing her mind? She was here for an interview, not to get gaga over some man's outward appearance.

Yet when she met his blue eyes, her mind went blank. They were as deep a blue as the Pacific on a sunny day. Alert and intelligent, they fixed on her. She swallowed hard, a frisson of alarm darting through her. Darn. Mr. Daniels hardly ever looked at her. She'd thought for sure busy businessmen were too preoccupied to pay attention to their office staff.

Matthew Gramling seemed to be the exception. His gaze missed nothing, from her plainly styled hair, gray of course, to the sensible pumps on her feet.

Once again she resisted the urge to double check her disguise.

"Mr. Gramling? I'm Miss Jones. We have an appointment at nine."

"Come in, Miss Jones. You are actually a few moments early." He paused a moment and then smiled. "I like that."

Karla nodded and swallowed hard. His smile caught her by surprise. The white teeth gleamed against his tanned skin. And the smile softened his features, making him look that much more approachable. That much more appealing. And sexy as could be!

She took a chair quickly, hoping she sat gracefully and didn't collapse just because her knees had suddenly grown weak. That smile should come with a warning—lethal to a woman's equilibrium!

She handed him the folder containing her résumé and sat back, trying her best to look confident and competent and ignore the way her pulse raced. Nerves, that was all.

It was a high-risk gamble, she knew that. But—aside from her looks—everything was the absolute truth. She'd worked on her résumé over the last week, polishing it until it showcased her experience and talents. Mr. Daniels had written her a wonderful letter of recommendation. Of course she had not told him of Mr. 25-50's views on employment. Her old boss had apparently never heard of Gramling's philosophy, so had no reason to suspect it would be more difficult to get the job than any other. His letter made no mention of age.

Matthew Gramling scanned the résumé, then placed it on his desk. Leaning back in his chair, he studied Karla.

"You've been working only eight years?" he asked.

"I decided when planning to join the work force to take a secretarial course so I'd be better able to compete with—'' she hesitated just a moment, hoping she was playing this right ''—younger women.'' Tilting her chin, she dared him to comment.

''All your experience has been with McCormick & Associates, I see.''

She nodded. ''A definite advantage wouldn't you say? I worked my way up, which shows they were pleased with my work. And I understand the ins and outs of Pacific Rim trade. I heard rumors you wish to expand Kinsinger Electronics into that arena. Mr. Daniels found me most valuable.''

''I plan to make changes in the firm, true,'' he said. He leaned back in his chair, but the pose was deceptive. Karla knew he remained alert to every nuance of their conversation.

''It would be odd if you didn't. I expect you have a lot of new ideas that will move the company ahead in the twenty-first century.''

''Moore ran it like a family business. I definitely plan to change that. Tell me something about your experiences at McCormick.''

The interview continued for more than forty-five minutes. Karla answered all questions honestly and with forethought. If he had asked her age, she would have told him without hesitation. He did not. If he thought she were older from the glasses she wore, the conservative clothing, the wig and the stage makeup that aged her skin, that was his problem.

She was convinced if she got the job, once he realized how competent she was, and that she had no intention of taking off on some romantic fantasy, he'd be willing to admit his odd notions of employee ages was faulty. But until then, she was willing to dress the part.

If she got the job.

"Do you have any questions?" he asked finally.

"You have covered everything perfectly. I would very much appreciate the opportunity to work for you."

He stood, offering his hand. "The Human Resources Department will be in touch one way or the other by the end of the week."

Karla shook hands briefly. His palm was warm against hers, his fingers long and strong. For a dazzling moment, her senses seemed to go into overload. She wondered what it would be like to have those fingers in her hair or stroking her skin.

She flushed, hoping color didn't noticeably stain her cheeks.

"Goodbye," she said abruptly and turned. She forced herself to walk calmly across the expanse of office when she really wanted to dash away and put some distance between them. She'd never felt so aware of a man before. And she'd better make sure she did not convey that awareness in any manner. She wanted the job. It sounded perfect—exciting, challenging, and affording the opportunity to work independently to a large degree. She could handle it. If she got the chance.

Closing the door behind her, she leaned against it for a moment in relief. The die was cast. Would she get the position or not? She'd done her best, now it was up to Matthew Gramling.

But, as she headed for the elevators, she truly hoped she'd be a part of the team he talked about building to lead this company into new areas and expanding it. What an exciting time it would be.

Karla was on tenterhooks all week. She had little to do at work with Mr. Daniels winding up his affairs. Helping out where she could in other departments, she noted nothing had been said about her own continued employment. She hurried home each afternoon to check her answering machine, having reprogrammed the outgoing message before the interview. It sounded staid and professional. Nothing like the usually irreverent jingles she changed weekly.

By Friday, Karla had given up. She knew from Pat—who had thought Karla was wasting her time by interviewing—that Matt Gramling had had a stream of applicants for the job during the week. Karla knew many of them would actually have decades of experience. Which didn't make her own eight years look so impressive. Hope was hard to maintain with nothing to feed it.

At three, the phone rang at her desk.

"The job's been filled," Pat said quietly.

Karla's heart sank. She'd so wanted it. Not only for the advancement of her career, but for the opportunities it had offered to learn a new business, be a part of the leadership forging new strategies for the next century.

"Oh. Well, thanks for calling to tell me."

"By you!" Pat shrieked. "I don't believe it, but he's hiring you! You're to start on Monday. How did you do it? I thought his 25-50 rule was firm. Wait until some of the other women in the company hear this!"

Karla felt almost giddy with reaction. She'd got the job! She'd done it!

Then what Pat said penetrated.

"Uh, Pat, wait! Don't say anything, please? I, um, actually, I think he believes I'm older than twenty-eight."

"Older? How much older?"

"I don't know. But at the interview, I, ah, had gray hair and a lot of wrinkles around my eyes and on my cheeks."

The silence on the other end stretched out for quite some time.

"You convinced him you're older?" Pat said at last.

"He never asked my age and I never volunteered it," Karla said, the first flush of excitement tempered by the knowledge she had to maintain that mature look for a while at least. Maybe for as long as she worked for him. Could she do it? For a moment the vision of twenty years of dressing older than she was danced before her.

She had to convince him, and quickly, that twenty-eight was a perfect age for an executive assistant!

"He'll know once he sees the employment papers, your age will be clearly listed there," Pat said slowly, as if having trouble taking in the situation.

"Ah." Frantically Karla tried to think. "Why does he need to see anything? You can just say Human Resources has taken care of everything. Impress him with your efficiency."

Pat giggled. "Good thing I'm leaving next week. I'd be out on my ear if he ever finds out. But why not? An unfair bias against age is wrong—whichever direction. I'll give it a shot. Anyway, congratulations. I guess. I hope you like the job as much as you think you will. I know you can handle it. That is, if you last the first day.

Honestly, Karla, this is the craziest scheme I've ever heard of.''

''It'll work. I'm sure of it. And I think I'll love the job,'' Karla said, then rang off, elated. She had done it! She started Monday morning as executive assistant to the new CEO of Kinsinger Electronics!

Now it remained to be seen if she could pull it off.

Matt Gramling loved a challenge, and pulling Kinsinger Electronics from the brink of bankruptcy and turning it into a dominant player in the Pacific Rim electronics industry was just the kind of challenge he loved. Some men had a talent for fishing, or acting or inventing. His was in turning around poorly run companies. And these days, he made sure he was the major shareholder before doing so.

He felt the familiar excitement build Monday morning. It was time to implement his ideas and strategies. See if he could pull the company from the brink of bankruptcy and make it a dominant player in its field.

He'd studied the reports generated by the department managers last week. They were in addition to the reports and projections his own people in Toronto had produced prior to the buyout. A firm grasp of the basic operation was crucial.

As was a good team. He glanced at his watch. It was still early. Today was Miss Jones's first day. He swiveled his chair until he could gaze out the window but didn't really see the waters of Coal Harbour dotted here and there with pleasure boats, or the dock where his floatation plane was moored with several others, or the tall trees of Stanley Park in the distance. The view of the Vancouver harbor was spectacular, but Matt ignored it, remembering their interview. He'd spoken with a dozen women last week, each more experienced and skilled than the last, it seemed. Yet there'd been something about the first one that had appealed to him. Her enthusiasm, maybe. Or her energy.

While she hadn't the breadth of experience some of the others had, she had worked at one firm her entire work career, which showed stability. If her boss hadn't retired, she wouldn't have been looking.

He wondered briefly what she'd done prior to that secretarial course. Raised a family, he'd bet. Had there been a divorce? Once the kids were grown, she'd gone into the work force?

It didn't matter. She was perfect—mature and sensible. She hadn't appeared the least bit flighty, and was too old to get moonstruck over some man. Or flirt with her boss. He'd be able to depend upon her as Daniels had. His letter had been straightforward and factual. Not the glowing testimony of some of the others, but solid. He trusted his instinct.

A noise in the outer office alerted him. Rising, he crossed to the door.

Miss Jones was putting away her purse. She looked up when he spoke.

"Good morning."

"Good morning, sir." She smiled. "Thank you for giving me the opportunity to work for you. I'll do my best."

"That's all I ask. When you've had a chance to settle in, bring a pad and we'll sort out how I like things run."

"Can I get you some coffee?" she asked.

"I picked up some earlier." He hesitated. Bringing coffee was something younger women objected to. He didn't need anyone to wait on him, but it was nice to have the offer made. "Do you want a chance to get a cup?"

"Oh, no, I'm ready now," she said, picking up two sharpened pencils and a pristine new notepad.

Matt held the door for her and stood aside as she preceded him into the office. It paid to hire the right people for the job. And here was someone who put work before coffee—ready to start even before eight! Strong validation for his choice.

She hesitated when she saw his desk. "Been working, I see," she murmured.

Matt walked around the desk, aware of the stacks of folders and printouts he'd been perusing since he arrived. He wanted her knowledgeable about the company as quickly as possible. She could review some of the reports as a kind of get-acquainted briefing.

"Some of this was from the weekend. I need to get up to speed as quickly as possible."

"I would have thought you'd know the company inside out before you bought it," she said, sitting in the chair opposite his and flipping open the notebook.

"I knew enough to know it was floundering and I could turn it around. In order to do that, now I need to know every little detail."

Matt sat in his chair and looked at her. Her gaze was on the notebook, pencil poised. She was going to be a gem!

"We'll start with my routine first. Then we'll get someone from Human Resources to give you a tour of the company. Introduce you around. Once you know the layout, you're welcomed to read some of the reports, to see what various departments do.''

"Perfect. Let me know what you expect of me, and what I can do to make things run more smoothly for you." She'd ask Pat to show her around. She'd get a lot of insider knowledge that way. She wished her friend would be staying at Kinsinger's, but she had already given notice, planning to stay home with her new baby.

He nodded. "First you need to hire a typist to do the basics—for drafts of reports and correspondence, filing, that kind of thing. I need your skills for other tasks. Then arrange to get a newer computer than the former assistant had and have these programs loaded." He tossed her a sheet of paper with the programs he used noted.

Leaning back, he began to tell her how he liked his day structured. Realizing interruptions were part and parcel of daily operations, he still expected her to field as many calls as she could. He indicated which aspects of the office he expected her to handle and which he'd see to himself.

It helped periodically to review the way he ran things. The operation in Toronto was now managed by his chief operating officer, Ted Clyde. With Kinsinger Electronics, he was starting fresh once again. And could structure the operations the way he thought best.

His respect for Miss Jones began to grow. She was quietly taking notes, asking an intelligent question now and then to clarify things. She didn't seem overwhelmed with the tasks he was delineating. Nor did she protest at the amount of work he piled on. She was going to be perfect.

"That's it. I'll leave it to you to get started on scheduling the managers in to see me."

"No problem."

That had been her standard response for everything. Matt almost smiled. He hoped none of it would be too much, he found he liked being around her. She brought with her a sense of serenity. Would it last? Or once they reached their stride, would she become as harried as Sarah Marling, his secretary in Toronto, always seemed? Time would tell.

"One last thing," he said.

She looked up. For a moment he felt a hint of awareness brush across him. Her eyes sparkled with enthusiasm behind her glasses. No makeup—except what seemed to be powder. She was not plain by any means—her bone structure was good. If her hair hadn't turned gray and wrinkles covered her skin, she'd still be an attractive woman. Her figure—

He frowned. He didn't usually give much thought to the personal aspects of his assistants.

"The work week will be erratic starting out. I'll demand a lot of after-hours' time initially—until I get things going the way I want—as quickly as I can."

"No problem."

He did smile at that. "And what would constitute a problem?" he asked.

Her eyes narrowed slightly. "Nothing I can think of right now, sir. If I come up with something, I'll let you know."

"I don't go for so much formality. You can call me Matt. I'll call you—"

His mind went blank. He knew he'd seen her first name on the résumé, what was it?

"Miss Jones," she said primly. Then cleared her throat, smiling a little. "Or Jeannette."

"Miss Jones? Not married?" Why hadn't he covered this in the interview? Hadn't most women her age been at least married once? Maybe she had been and took back her maiden name after a divorce.

She shook her head once.

"Ever been?"

"How does that impact my work here?" she asked sharply.

"It doesn't. I was out of line, Miss Jones. Jeannette. I apologize."

Out of line, maybe, but curious. Had he hit a hot button? Not that it mattered. She worked for him now and that was what was important, not her private life.

"I'll see to this," she said, indicating the list of notes she'd jotted down.

He watched her walk from the office. For a moment he wanted to ask her to stay—to talk for a moment—to learn more about the woman he'd hired.

Time enough to learn more about her as they worked together. He already knew all he needed to start. But the curiosity lingered.

CHAPTER TWO

KARLA felt as if she'd been running a marathon by the end of work on Friday. Matt Gramling was a high-energy person from the get-go. No matter how early she arrived at work, he was already in his office—freshly attired and raring to plunge into the day's activities.

And she knew the description of slave driver wasn't far off. Yet, how could she complain when he worked so hard himself—harder than anyone else at the firm.

She stayed late three nights during the week, not getting home on Wednesday until well after midnight. Yet she knew he had to stay even later every night, with the fresh stack of work that always awaited her each morning.

She was tired beyond belief. How did he think an older woman would have kept up with his pace?

Not that she would ask. Or give any hint things weren't going along perfectly. She was determined to do her best with this job and prove to him his notions of employee ages were faulty.

And it appeared to be the only faulty thing about the man.

Besides incredible energy, he had exciting ideas to grow the business. New ways to view old techniques and policies—and innovative methods in dealing with personnel.

He engendered an excitement throughout the company

that was infectious. From the administrative offices to the plant on the outskirts of the city, morale was on the rise.

Department after department became caught up in the new wave of ideas and changes. Managers arrived at his office in trepidation—fearful of what he'd find wrong with their departments. They left refreshed and inspired by the new ideas discussed. For the most part, that is. Two managers were given notice, and one put on alert his department had to change for the better, or he'd be gone.

Karla watched daily, amazed she could actually feel the energy level throughout the entire organization rise.

She and Pat had time for a quick lunch on Thursday, but beyond that, she'd been at her desk nonstop. Except for the times Matt spent with her. Sometimes they'd get off topic and discussed philosophical aspects of running a business. He seemed to listen attentively to her views, which proved delightfully appealing when he had so much more success in business than she.

At five on Friday, she straightened her stacks of folders, wondering if she dare leave. She should check with Matt once more before taking off for the weekend. She had a date with her friend Kevin Fowler to attend a new musical. If she needed to cancel, she'd want to give him as much notice as possible.

Matt had mentioned to her earlier that morning that he was leaving for the weekend, so she knew there'd be no required work Saturday and Sunday. She planned to sleep in late tomorrow!

But did he have any last-minute tasks to take care of today?

Duty called.

She stepped into the open doorway to his office. "If you have nothing further for me, Mr. Gramling, I'll be leaving."

He looked up, then glanced at his watch. "No, nothing that can't wait until Monday. I'm glad you let me know the time. I have something going on tonight."

Karla nodded impersonally, wondering if it were a hot date. She had noticed during the week a certain number of calls he'd received from women that seemed to have nothing to do with business. He must be a fast worker, she knew he'd only been in Vancouver a couple of weeks.

Not that it was any of her concern.

He tossed down his pen and leaned back in his chair. "So how did your first week go?" he asked.

"I liked it. It was different from what I expected."

"And that was?"

"I didn't anticipate so much autonomy, for one thing. I appreciate your giving me the chance to make decisions right off the bat."

"Why not, you handled everything perfectly."

She smiled, taking pride in his compliment. "Not a problem," she murmured.

He laughed. "I'll wait for the day you announce a problem. Have a nice weekend, Miss Jones. I'll see you early Monday."

"And you, Mr. Gramling."

Despite his repeatedly reminding her to call him Matt, she wanted the barrier of formality between them. Sometimes he called her Jeannette, and she had to remember to respond. She was not used to answering to her middle name.

Their morning meetings worked to strengthen the bond growing between them. She knew in a few months she would be so attuned to his way of dealing with situations that she would be able to predict his reaction. Her hope was he'd feel the same about his executive assistant.

She hurried home and into the shower. Washing away the stage makeup each day was such a relief. And to be able to run her fingers through her short dark hair was also a delight she wouldn't take for granted anytime soon.

The shower refreshed her and she was ready when Kevin showed up promptly at six-thirty. They were grabbing a quick bite then going to the performance.

The musical had been playing to a sellout crowd. Kevin bragged about pulling in a favor to obtain great seats, near the center close to the front. Karla sat down with relief. For the next hour, she could sit and veg out— enjoy the entertainment and not have to be "on." Conversing with Kevin during dinner had been a strain despite their longtime friendship. Normally she liked spending time with him. But tonight, she was too tired. She should have begged off the evening, but knew he'd gone to a lot of trouble to get the tickets. And she'd been looking forward to seeing the show. If she could keep her eyes open!

Twice during the performance she caught herself in a huge yawn. Once, her head nodded as she almost dozed off.

Flicking a glance at Kevin, she was relieved he hadn't noticed. It wasn't his fault she was so tired.

She looked beyond him—and her heart stopped. Matthew Gramling was staring at her from two rows over.

Karla quickly looked away, her heart pounding. Fatigue fled. Good grief, what was he doing here?

What was she going to do? Had he recognized her? She lost track of the performance as thoughts tumbled around in her mind. Surreptitiously, she peeked in his direction again. He seemed engrossed in the antics of the actors on stage. The seat next to him was vacant. Then, as if he'd been touched on the shoulder, he glanced her way again.

She swung her head back to face the stage. Why was he looking at her?

She shifted a bit, her delight in the musical dimmed. Glancing casually over her shoulder, she met his gaze. Hoping she hadn't given herself away, she slowly looked away, wishing she could sink beneath the seats! He was staring at her! He must have recognized her. But how? Her hair, makeup, dress—everything—was different. It was dark in the theater, was he just suspicious? Or did he know for certain?

Could she plead a headache and get Kevin to take her home early? Escape before Matt had a chance to confirm his suspicions?

No, that wasn't fair to Kevin. He had every right to expect to enjoy the entire performance. What was she going to do?

After one week, Karla knew she wanted to work for Kinsinger for a long time. It was the perfect job! Was she going to get fired here at the theater a mere five days into her new career?

She let several minutes pass before peeking around. Matt was watching the show—no, he glanced her way and caught her gaze. Drat the man, couldn't he become engrossed in the musical? She looked straight ahead, wondering how long before she could escape.

At the intermission, Kevin offered to get them drinks.

"White wine?" he asked as they slowly moved up the long aisle, buffeted by the other theatergoers heading for the lobby.

"Just sparkling water tonight, please. I'm so tired I'd fall asleep if I drank anything alcoholic," she said. Glancing around the crowded lobby, she didn't see Matt. There were a lot of people—what were the odds they'd run into each other? Motioning to a quiet corner, she smiled at Kevin. "I'll wait there, if that's all right with you. I don't want to fight the crowd tonight."

"Good idea. I'll be back as quick as I can."

She cut across the flow of patrons and found the eddy of peace. What she should have done was stayed in her seat and taken a quick catnap. Or pleaded a headache and fled the theater to make sure she didn't run into her boss.

Another yawn came. She covered her mouth with her hand and gave in. She hoped she'd stay awake until she could get home. It wasn't fair to Kevin to be so tired he couldn't enjoy the evening.

"Can I get you a cup of coffee?" a familiar voice asked.

Startled, Karla swung to her left, and came face-to-face with Matt Gramling!

So much for trying to avoid him.

Stunned, she couldn't speak. What was he doing here? Had he deliberately sought her out?

"I, um," she stammered. Had he followed her? No, that was dumb—unless he *did* suspect and had come to uncover her deception.

"Sorry, I couldn't help notice you seem tired." Dressed in a dark suit and fresh shirt, he looked wonderful. Karla had to force her gaze away.

"I am a bit tired," she said shortly.

Scanning the crowd, he frowned slightly. "Weren't you with someone?"

She nodded, trying to capture some semblance of rationality. Taking a deep breath, she hoped she could calm her nerves. He hadn't recognized her—at least he hadn't instantly denounced her, or demanded an explanation. Was it just coincidence?

Swinging back to look at her, he smiled, and held out his hand. "I'm Matt Gramling. New in town. Are you enjoying the show, or too tired to appreciate it?"

She took his hand, releasing it as quickly as she could without causing comment. The same spark that she remembered from the interview seemed to flow up her arm. That same sexy smile had her knees feeling decidedly wobbly, and that same intensity he brought to bear on the job front showed as he gazed down at her as if they were the only two people in the theater.

"I'm, uh, Karla. And the show's great."

He'd think she didn't even know her own name the way she stammered. Better that than the truth—her nerves were stretched to the limit. Not only by the fear of exposure, but by the wild feelings that rose being so near him.

"Nice to meet you, Karla. Did you get stranded?"

"Stranded? Oh, no. Kevin went to get us something to drink. I didn't want to face the crowds."

"Coffee, I hope?"

She shook her head, glancing up to be caught by his

gaze, feeling mesmerized by his eyes. They remained focused solely on her. As a technique for making someone feel important, it was dynamite! Her heart raced and her thoughts spun.

So these were the plans he had for the evening. Good thing she hadn't told him of her own plans. She almost shivered at the close call.

"Are you here alone?" she asked, wondering how long it would be before some jealous woman came up and snatched him away. Yet the seat next to his had been vacant.

"My date came down sick just before we were due to leave, and I didn't want to waste both tickets. It was too late by then to call someone else."

He was alone—and trying to pick her up?

"Do you know me?" she asked warily. Was she reading the signs correctly? Any other time she'd have been delighted to meet such a personable man. Of all the luck.

"I don't know, do I? You look familiar. I saw you earlier in the theater."

Several times, she thought. Had he thought she was flirting with him?

"I'm sure I would have remembered if we had met before," she said, stalling for time. Where was Kevin? Things were getting complicated.

"While you appear to be enjoying the show, you also look tired. Tough day?" he asked.

"Tough week."

He tilted his head a moment as if listening more intently. His eyes narrowed as he studied her. "You look very familiar. Even your voice sounds familiar."

Oops, if he recognized nothing else, would he recognize her voice?

She lowered it slightly, rushing into speech, "Sorry about your date. The show is funny and I love the way that song at the beginning burst forth. I expect the CD sales will be terrific."

She glanced away as her mind went blank. What else could she say? Her heart raced. She had never in a million years expected to run into Matt without her disguise. Vancouver was a big city, what were the odds?

"How serious are you and the man you're with?" he asked abruptly.

She swung back, startled. "Kevin? We're friends. Have been for years."

"Do you ever expand your circle of friends?"

Slowly Karla began to smile. He was trying to pick her up. It gave her an entirely new view of her boss.

"It depends," she said.

He definitely hadn't recognized her! Of course with her own short dark hair, the lack of aging makeup, wig and glasses—not to mention the fun, flirty dress she wore—probably no one would recognize the staid Miss Jones.

He glanced around again—looking for Kevin? she wondered.

"I have to go out of town this weekend, but I'll call you when I get back," he said, bringing his focus back to her. "We could have dinner together one night this week." He raised an eyebrow in question.

Karla's mind went totally blank. She stared at him, wondering why fate had decided to give her the job, then snatch it away in such an unlikely manner.

"Karla? Would you have dinner with me one night this week?" he repeated.

Her thoughts whirling, she opened her mouth to refuse. Then snapped it shut and gave him a polite smile, feeling like her face would crack. "I, um, I'm not sure of my schedule."

"Busy lady," he murmured. "I'll call you and you can check."

Idiot, she told herself. You should have pretended Kevin was the love of your life. How was she going to gracefully get out of this mess?

"If you give me your phone number," he said when she remained silent.

Had he already asked her that? Hesitantly, she gave him the number of her cell phone. Was she playing with fire? She wasn't sure he'd call, much less that she'd go through with a date. She could say she was busy.

Then she almost laughed. Did he realize she was older than his dating limit? She'd often been told she looked younger than her age. Maybe she should mention she was twenty-eight and nip this in the bud.

"Karla, there you are." Kevin joined them, balancing two full glasses. He handed her one. "As requested."

He looked inquiringly at Matt.

"Kevin Fowler, this is Matt Gramling. A new... acquaintance," Karla said, with a provocative look at Matt. She was feeling much more secure. And it was unlikely he'd ever call.

"Matt." Kevin shook hands. "Enjoying the performance?"

"Very much, now," he said.

Karla sipped her sparkling water, aware of a tingling

sensation dancing across her skin. All thoughts of fatigue had fled. There was no denying just being around Matt— whether at work or in the lobby of a crowded theater— had her wide awake and alert.

And again very aware of him as a man. What would it be like to go out together? To spend some time talking about non-business topics. To learn more about the complex man who now headed Kinsinger Electronics.

The lights flickered, indicating time to return to their seats.

"I'll be in touch," Matt promised.

She watched him stride away, soon caught up in the swirl of bodies moving back into the theater. For a second the evening went flat. Then she smiled at Kevin. He was a nice man who had been her friend for years. She usually enjoyed going out with him, they had fun and there was no pressure. Neither felt any spark with the other, so their relationship was uncluttered by sexual overtones.

But something told her going out with Matt Gramling—if she dared—would not provide the easy-going companionship being with Kevin did. There were definitely sexual overtones—in spades. Was she the only one to notice?

Knowing Matt planned to be gone all weekend, Karla didn't expect to hear from him. When her cell phone rang early Sunday afternoon, she was surprised. Snatching it from her purse, she flipped it open.

"Hello?"

"Karla? Matt Gramling. I said I'd call."

"So you did." She sat on the sofa, a silly grin spreading on her face. "I also thought you said you'd be out of town this weekend."

"I was. Just got back."

And called her first thing? That gave her food for thought.

"Where were you?" she asked.

"I have access to a cabin up on Henley Island. I flew up to check it out. It'll come in handy to get away from the city when things get hectic at work."

She knew from the paperwork she'd seen during the past week that he owned and piloted his own floatation plane. If she had a view of the harbor, she might have been able to watch him take off or land this weekend. The shuttle planes routinely used the harbor, but private planes were rare.

"And is it nice?"

"It'll do. Are you free this afternoon? Since I got back earlier than originally planned, I thought you could show me around a bit and I'll buy you dinner."

Warning bells clanged. Karla knew better than to tempt fate. How long could she ever expect to keep two personas separate if she flaunted both of them at Matt?

But the idea of spending some time with him outside of the company tantalized. He was a fascinating and complex individual. Wouldn't it help at work to understand him better? And he wasn't asking for anything more than sight-seeing and dinner. She'd probably be home by eight.

"Okay," she said. "Where shall I meet you?"

"I'll come pick you up," he said.

Definitely not a good idea.

"How about I meet you at Canada Place? Do you know where that is?"

"Of course. It's near where I have my plane moored."

Canada Place was a landmark in Vancouver—the embarkation point for all the cruise lines that stopped on their way to and from Alaska.

"Say in thirty minutes?"

It wouldn't take her that long to get there, but she did have to change and do something about her hair!

"It's windy today, dress warmly," he said.

She clicked off the phone, giddy with anticipation. Darting into the bedroom, she flung open the closet door and almost groaned. What would be suitable for a casual afternoon, warm—and also be appropriate for dinner later?

If he was serious about seeing the sights, it wouldn't matter. She drew her shirt over her head and snagged a yellow sweater. Pulling it on, she fluffed her hair.

Makeup, definitely. She applied carefully, hoping she looked far, far different from Miss Jones.

And forget glasses—even sunglasses. She didn't want to give him a hint to remind him of her alter persona.

Ready in fifteen minutes, she let herself out of her flat and walked briskly toward the waterfront. The air was crisp and clean. The sun shone in a cloudless sky. The wind was cool, holding a tang of salt as it blew in from the water. As she drew near the rendezvous point, she could feel her heart rate increase in anticipation.

Karla spotted him long before he saw her. She watched as he leaned against the railing, studying the pleasure boats in the water. He checked his watch once or twice.

In the office he had the patience of Job. Was he impatiently waiting to see her?

She almost skipped with delight. Then stopped dead. Was she an idiot? She could blow everything with a careless word, or even a hint of similarity between herself and "Miss Jones."

Matt looked up and spotted her—his eyes narrowed as he watched her slowly approach. What was he thinking? she wondered. Then she forgot to think as his gaze drew her closer.

"Hi," Karla said when she drew near. The worry of exposure jumped to the forefront of her mind.

"Hi, yourself." His gaze traveled down the jacket, over the bright yellow sweater and down the long legs encased in snug black pants.

Karla let her own gaze drift over Matt. The thick cable-knit sweater lovingly encased broad shoulders, tapering to a narrow waist. His own dark cords added to the casual look. Glancing up, she smiled. His hair looked great wind-tossed and sun-burnished. Just as she'd wanted to see it. She just wished she could brush it with her fingertips—just once—to see what it felt like.

Feeling as if she were balancing on a tightrope stretched across Capilano Canyon, she threw caution to the wind. She'd have her afternoon, and do her best to make sure he never connected her with his superior secretary!

"So you want to see Vancouver, huh? Where are you from?" She hoped she didn't get her facts mixed up—in which persona she was learning things.

"Toronto most recently." He turned and they started walking along the seawalk. The wide pedestrian path was dotted here and there with others strolling in the balmy afternoon sunshine.

"I've never been there. I bet it isn't any prettier than Vancouver," she said, loyal to her birthplace.

"It's different. This is a beautiful city. Tell me what you think I should see first."

"You can't see it all in one day," she warned. "Especially starting out this late."

"Then maybe you'll take pity on me and offer a second tour."

She grinned. "I suspect pity is the last thing you ever need. You seem more the bold pirate type to me."

He took her hand and placed it in the crook of his elbow, covering her fingers with his. "I go after what I want," he said.

Her heart skidded, began to pound. She'd seen his business side, now she was getting a full blast from the personal side. The way his fingers caressed hers set her pulse pounding, her skin tingling and her mind doing somersaults. How could anyone keep things straight when going into sensory overload?

"Then we have something in common," she said. "I do, too."

She glanced up at him from beneath her lashes and smiled a slow, provocative smile. "Let's start with Stanley Park, shall we?"

"I'm in your hands."

She wished for a moment that was true. Hadn't she fantasized about being in his? Shaking off the memories of her daydreams, Karla began to relate what she knew about the famous park at the edge of the city. He stopped her after a few moments, saying he hadn't invited her out to be a tour guide.

"And what are you looking for?" she asked.

"I'll know it when I see it. How about just a friend for now."

He was flirting with her, that she could tell. She liked it even though it meant nothing. After today, if she were smart, she wouldn't see him again. She'd have to decide—her job or a flirtation with Matt Gramling.

Her career was too important to risk.

"So tell me something about Matt Gramling," she invited. Something I don't already know, she thought. Something special just for me.

"Born and raised in the east. Moved here two weeks ago. Though I've visited Vancouver in the past."

She looked up at him. "That's all? How succinct. No family, no ties?"

His face took on a hard look. "No family. No ties."

"Everyone has family—either a birth family or one made later."

"I don't."

"Why not?"

His expression grew cold. "My parents are dead. I had no brothers or sisters."

"So you've become part of an extended family with close friends, a wife, kids."

He shook his head. "It's never happened and it won't."

Karla grew quiet at the remoteness in his tone. Everyone had family, she thought. What had happened to shut him off from others? The closed look to his face ended her inquiries on that topic. But her curiosity rose.

Sooner or later, if they kept seeing each other, she'd open the topic again. She was close to her family, couldn't imagine anyone not having someone.

As the silence grew, Karla began to talk about inane things to fill the void. By the time they reached the Totem Poles in Stanley Park, Matt had thawed enough to ask questions. Things seemed on an even keel again when they stopped to examine the Indian carvings.

Karla was congratulating herself on the success of the afternoon when he looked at her and said, "I figured it out, you know."

Catching her breath, she looked at him, hoping her expression gave nothing away. "Figured what out? How the Indians carved them?"

"Who you are."

Her heart skidded, then seem to stop. Only one week, it wasn't enough. She loved her new job, had wanted to work there for years—not be exposed after only one week. It wasn't fair!

"And that is?" She hoped her voice sounded right—slightly interested, intrigued even. She'd go down fighting.

"Miss Jeannette Jones's niece."

She blinked. "Jeannette Jones's niece?"

"The resemblance is remarkable. It came to me after we parted at the theater the other night."

She swallowed hard. "Oh?"

He nodded.

"How do you know Jeannette Jones?" she almost stammered, stalling for time. What was she going to do? How much of a leap was it from that to the truth?

"She started work for me last week. And since she's

single and never been married, I figured you had to be
her niece, right? The resemblance is almost uncanny. Of
course, she's quite a few years older.''

Karla looked at the Totem Poles wishing they could
provide her with the answer to his question. Did she go
along with his idea, or confess all?

She definitely should not have accepted his invitation
today.

''So you're the hotshot executive who's going to turn
Kinsinger Electronics into a major player in the electronics field,'' she said, trying to bluff her way through. If
she got home without discovery, she'd never risk it again!

''I plan to—with the help of people like your aunt.
She's a great addition to the company.''

Karla forced a smile, wishing she'd never started this
convoluted plan. And she was playing with fire trying to
see him personally. Was she crazy?

''That's good to hear.'' She smiled involuntarily.
Would he ever tell Jeannette that to her face?

''Come by the office next week. I'll take you and your
aunt out to lunch.''

CHAPTER THREE

KARLA had a life-size picture of that! Quickly she tried to come up with an excuse—without clueing him in. Maybe she could say she was being transferred—to Nova Scotia. Or that she worked nights and had to sleep days. Or there was a family feud and she and her aunt weren't speaking.

"I'll have to see," she said when the silence had gone on almost too long to not be noticeable. The last thing she wanted was for him to suspect anything. "Would you like to see the rose gardens?"

"I'd rather head back toward Gas Town, and get an early dinner. I didn't have any lunch and the walk and all this fresh air has made me hungry."

"Gas Town, huh? Have you seen it?" she asked. The older part of the city was a favorite spot of tourists, and some of the more carefree of Vancouver's citizens. Full of trendy shops, pubs and restaurants, it was a favorite area of the city for Karla.

"The flat I've sublet for a few months is nearby. I've eaten in the district almost every night since I arrived."

"Maybe you need some variety."

"A home-cooked meal?" he asked. "I wouldn't turn one down."

"Then let's hope someone offers you one," she said, sidestepping the issue, and starting back toward the center of town. All she wanted to do was get dinner over with and get back to the safety of her flat where she would swear off a dual existence forever!

"I thought you might be that someone," he said provocatively.

She shrugged, though the thought of him coming to her apartment, hovering over her while she prepared dinner, was tantalizing. "Maybe one day." When pigs flew. Or when the masquerade was over and everything aboveboard.

"I'll hold you to that."

The wind from the sea had picked up as the afternoon waned. It was cooler walking back along the seawalk. As if in one mind, they both picked up the pace.

"Tell me about your seaplane," she asked as she spotted several moored in the harbor.

He looked at her sharply. "How did you know I have a floatation plane?"

"You mentioned it when I asked if you knew where Canada Place was. Have you had it a long time?"

"A few years. I bought it to get away to some of the remote spots in the Yukon. I can land on a lake and not have to worry about finding an airport."

"The Yukon? Do you hunt and fish?"

"Occasionally—but only to catch dinner. I fly to the wilderness to escape the trappings of civilization. Camping gives me a release. Ever try it?"

She shook her head. "It must be fun, a lot of people seem to do it." She was starting to feel a bit breathless with their pace. Matt's legs were longer than hers and she was hard-pressed to keep up.

"I don't know about fun, but it's the best stress reducer I know. Using the plane, I can fly into spots where no one has been in years. Hiking and exploring some of the last wilderness areas gives me a chance to relax. My best business ideas come at the end of a long weekend off by myself.''

"Man against nature?"

"You could say that. It hones skills most men have lost living in a city."

"Doesn't it worry you that you'll get stranded or something catastrophic might happen so far from civilization?"

He shrugged. "I like being challenged, and overcoming odds."

She nodded—it figured. Hadn't she seen him as more than just a businessman? There was a latent restlessness about him. Being confined in the office every day wasn't his natural milieu. He appeared more real today, striding into the wind, with the sea beside him and the wind tossing his hair.

"Obviously no family in the picture," Karla murmured, thankful to spot the edge of Gas Town. The steam clock clearly visible in the distance. "They'd be worried sick if you took off for long without a way to communicate."

He shrugged. "As I said earlier, none in the picture present or future."

"You can't discount the future. Don't you plan to get married?"

"No, I don't plan to get married. How about you, anxious to tie the knot?"

She shook her head. "Nuh, uh. Not for a long, long time."

"That's surprising, most women I know can't wait to

get married—preferably to the man with the biggest bank account.''

"Wow, Cynics-R-Us. Maybe you're hanging around the wrong women," Karla said, taken aback at the vehemence in his tone.

"You're saying you wouldn't marry a man who had a big bank account?"

"I'm not sure a bank account is anything I'd care about at the onset. Don't you think compatibility and love should count somewhere in there?"

"Love? A purely feminine concept to cover the more honest emotion of lust. Which, once it moves on, leaves nothing!"

"Good grief, you *are* a cynic. Who burned you?"

He stopped at the traffic signal. Looking at her, Matt narrowed his eyes. "Once a long time ago a woman promised love and devotion. We were planning to marry—until she found out the size of my bank account compared to a friend's. It didn't take long for her to correct her mistake. So much for love and devotion."

"And you were so hurt you won't chance your heart again," Karla murmured.

"No. I was never in love, as you say. Celine and I enjoyed each other's company, she was good in bed. But once she showed her true colors, I moved on. Only this time, wiser to the ploys of women."

"Sounds like you got a lucky escape. But not all women are like that, greedy for money and not the man. Most women marry for love."

"I'd expect you to say that. Who wants to admit to being mercenary?"

"At least I didn't disappoint you," she retorted. "So

because of one bad experience, you've sworn off women?''

''No. I like women. I enjoy being with them. I've enjoyed being with you today. I've sworn off marriage.''

''Do you want to grow old all alone?''

''If that begins to bother me in my declining years, I'll buy a wife. You're a fine one to talk. There's no wedding ring on your finger.''

''I didn't swear off marriage, but it's not something I'm looking for at the moment. Besides, I haven't met the right man.''

''You call me cynical. But with those rose-colored glasses you wear, I'm surprised you can walk around without bumping into buildings. How will you recognize *the right man?*''

Karla began to cross the street when the light changed, wondering how seriously Matt wished to hear her views.

''I would expect there would be some attraction between us.''

Like the instant attraction she seemed to feel whenever she was around Matt? Heck, she didn't have to be around him, she could just think about him and feel weightless.

That thought made her pause. ''Of course we'd have to have a lot in common,'' she rushed to add. ''Likes and interests shared, that kind of thing. And I think our goals should be the same—both want the same thing from a marriage.''

''And what if you meet some guy who's a bum, and there's that lighting strike of attraction? You're telling me you'd pursue it? I don't think so.''

She laughed. ''Matt, I'm not going to find some bum and fall for him.''

"Because of his bank balance."

"Because I don't hang out where bums hang out. I also don't hang out where the really rich do, either. So the chances of finding and falling for a really rich guy are somewhere between slim and none. Get real."

He indicated a small restaurant, holding the door for her. Inside it was dark and modest, with few people occupying the tables. It was early, more tables would fill up later.

"It doesn't look like much, but the food's terrific," he said.

"I like pubs," she said, taking in the dark walls and large chairs. It didn't take long to be seated, and soon Karla was avidly studying the menu. The fresh air had caused her to work up an appetite.

Ordering shepard's pie, she looked at Matt, wondering if he planned to take up the discussion about matrimony again. His views were controversial, and a bit sad.

She wondered who the woman had been who had scorned him for his rich friend. And if she had any clue of the havoc she left in her wake. Was he protesting too much, or did he really not feel hurt any longer because of that woman's defection? Guys rarely expressed feelings like that. And she suspected Matt was more reticent than most.

He looked up and caught her gaze. "One of the things that caught my eye with you I saw at the play. You were with a date, but not hanging over him. Not trying to pretend you were the only person in the theater he should acknowledge."

"Kevin and I are friends, nothing more."

"Then I want us to become friends. But nothing more.

I suspected we might have something in common—a dislike of ties.''

"I don't dislike ties.''

"I phrased it wrong. You are not looking for a husband, right?''

She hesitated a moment. "Not now, at least.''

"Knowing from the onset that there is no chance of a long-term relationship should keep things from getting sticky later.''

She almost smiled. "You mean when we stop seeing each other?''

"I hate clinging women.''

"And I would have said earlier that I disliked egotistical men. But I find you—'' she tilted her head to the left, considering "—fascinating. You might want to work on that arrogance, however.''

His eyes gleamed with humor.

"Want to work on it yourself?''

"Whoa, that's a tempting offer.''

"Do we have a deal?''

She hesitated a moment. What of her commitment to stay as far from him as she could during non-working hours? Wasn't she playing with fire to see him again? But the afternoon had been so much fun—all from spending time with him.

"Deal. No entanglements for either of us! Friends only.''

She dare not get too close—not if she wanted to keep her job with Kinsinger. He had nothing to worry about. Today would give them an idea of the limit of their involvement, she thought, as the waiter approached their table. They could talk, do things together, and share a meal. But nothing more!

"So, tell me how a closet woodsman became head of an electronics firm," she said once their orders had been taken.

He leaned back in his chair, stretching out his long legs beneath the table. He brushed against Karla. Deliberately? Awareness flooded through her at his touch. After he'd released her hand on their walk, she'd made sure they hadn't touched again. It was easier to pay attention to what was going one without her body going haywire from direct contact.

She didn't move, fearing he'd read more into the gesture than was warranted. Hadn't she tried to match his own detachment? But she was fully aware of the warmth emanating from his leg, of the tingling waves of excitement. Swallowing hard, she tried to focus on what he was saying and ignore the sensations that raced through her.

"I had to work my way through college. My sophomore year, I got a job at a rundown printing firm. They were barely making ends meet, and tried to cut corners by hiring the lowest-paid workers they could. One day, I made a suggestion to the manager. He thought about it for a while then implemented it. In less than two months, they started turning a profit for the first time in years."

She smiled, she was such a sucker for a happy ending. "So you were the hero of the hour. Had you studied business economics in college? Were you applying course work?"

He shook his head. "I was still in the basic breadth course work stage, hadn't had any business courses yet.

It was a gut feel, common sense, as I saw it. But it taught me one important fact.''

"And that was?''

"That not everyone in business has that common sense approach. And not a lot of people are willing to take risks on gut feelings.''

"But you are.''

"I am.''

"So the company became a success?''

He nodded.

"Did you get a raise?''

Matt hesitated a moment, then a gleam shone in his eye. "Actually, I ended up getting partial ownership, and really studied the dynamics of the company. By the time I graduated from the university, I'd changed the entire way it was run, and it was making money hand over fist. It still brings in a hefty annual return.''

"So a businessman was born. What did you do next?''

He sat up when the waiter arrived with their meal, waiting until he left before looking back at Karla.

She missed the warmth from his leg when he changed positions. But at least she could concentrate more fully on what he was saying without the zinging electrical current zapping through her. She took a deep breath, hoping to keep her hormones under control. They were merely acquaintances who were sharing dinner. Nothing more. Matt had made sure his views were known. If a woman was foolish enough to think she'd get more, she had only herself to blame if he broke off early.

Karla knew she wasn't foolish enough to expect more than a casual date now and again. But that would be enough. She could learn more about her boss, and hopefully find ways to work more smoothly with him because of it.

And find ways to ignore the tingling attacks that happened only around Matt.

"There has to be more interesting things to discuss than my business background."

"Not to me," she said, fascinated by this glimpse of the man she'd been working with for a week. It gave her an idea of how he'd become so successful. The drive and determination were ingrained. She had a lot to learn from him. But more importantly, she wanted to glean every bit of knowledge she could about this fascinating man to satisfy her feminine curiosity.

"What do you do? I'll see if I can tell you some stories that would tie in with your own career."

Karla's mind went absolutely blank. She stared at him, conscious of the way his hair was still a bit wind-tossed, of the breadth of his shoulders in the sweater, of the focus of those clear blue eyes.

"I'm a secretary," she said finally. Please don't let him ask where.

"Like your aunt?"

She hesitated, then shrugged. Actually her only aunt was a veterinarian, but Matt didn't have to know that. He thought she was her own aunt.

"Where?"

"At a small firm near the financial district. I want to hear more about your career. You didn't just leave the printing firm for the electronics one, did you? What did you do between the university and now?"

She picked up her fork and took a bite of food. She couldn't talk if she were eating. She hoped he'd take the question seriously and tell her more. She liked listening to him talk. His voice was deep and dark. For a second, she wondered how it would sound whispering words of passion and love.

She choked on her food and quickly reached for her water glass. She refused to give in to fantasies about this man. Tonight was a one-off deal. Hereafter she'd do better to stick to work and not give in to temptation to spend personal time with him. If he ever even called again.

He began to cut the steak he'd ordered, glancing at her when she coughed. "Are you all right?"

She nodded, sipping the water to calm her throat.

"Tell me what happened after the printer's," she said when she could speak again. This time she'd keep her thoughts firmly on what he was saying and not daydream about hearing his voice in the dark!

"I found from that first place that I had an aptitude for turning around troubled situations. Once I had a bit of money set aside, I went looking to see if I could repeat what I'd done. Or if it were a fluke."

"It wasn't. I just bet you've been totally successful right from the start." She couldn't wait to hear the next success tale.

"Yes and no. The next venture was in sporting goods. A retail store in Toronto. That took a bit longer to turn around. And it was then I met Celine."

"Celine?"

"The woman I asked to marry me."

"Oh." Karla was dying to hear all about her. But hadn't a clue how to get him to talk without appearing blatantly curious.

She waved her hand dismissingly. "She sounds like a fool anyway."

"Why?"

"Choosing someone else over you."

He studied Karla over the table.

She looked up and met his gaze, feeling that same tingling sensation she'd felt when his leg had brushed against hers.

"What?"

"An interesting observation from someone who professes not to be interested in a long-term relationship—or marriage. Why was she a fool?"

She laughed. "Get real. I bet since she dumped you that you've made a mint. Nothing like wanting to better someone for strictly personal reasons to goad a person to achieve new highs. You probably out-earn your former friend hand over fist. If Celine knew, she'd be furious with herself."

"Not interested in bank accounts?" he said silkily.

"Come on, Matt, it's obvious. If you've done well in the first firm when you were so young, you probably did better in your next venture with experience behind you. Don't you think it only makes sense? You've done printing, sporting goods and security systems, now electronics. Obviously you know what you're doing, and with each success you can, and I bet do, demand a bigger piece of the pie. I know that much about how business works."

He put down his fork. "How did you know about the security systems?"

Karla's heart stopped for a second. "You told me," she said brazenly. He had, but not today, she realized.

She knew because he was still involved with the company in Toronto and, as Jeannette Jones, she'd had access to that information. "It's the firm you just left behind in Toronto."

God, she would never pull this off! He'd know instantly he hadn't mentioned it today. It wouldn't take him two seconds to guess where she'd learned it—then fire her on the spot.

Matt looked away, as if thinking. Karla took another sip of water, wondering how long it would be before he—

"I'm more tired than I thought. I don't remember talking about it."

"If you're tired from your weekend, we can eat quickly and call it a day," she said. What had started as a lark was proving to be more of a strain than she expected. Especially when she made a glaring faux pas like that one.

If she could just make it safely through, she vowed, she would not challenge fate again. It would be strictly business only from now on.

"I didn't think I was that tired," he said dryly. "At least I'm not yawning openly like you were last Friday night."

She cringed. "Please, let's forget that evening. I can't believe I almost dozed off during the production. I do try to get enough rest—like getting in early on Sundays," she said, trying to change the subject before he examined it further. "I have a busy week ahead and still have to get my clothes lined up for the week. I've had a great time this afternoon, but do need to go home soon so I can wash my hair and all." She was babbling, she knew it, but all she wanted to do was end the evening as quickly as possible before disaster fell.

Matt nodded gravely. ''I can see that washing your hair would take a long time.''

She blushed and began eating with gusto. Her short hair took no time to wash and dry. It was the easiest style to care for.

''Meet me for lunch tomorrow,'' Matt said.

''Can't, Monday's my busiest day.''

''Tuesday, then?''

She met his eyes and shrugged. ''I'll have to check my calendar at work. I don't get a long lunch hour.'' And if he pushed, she'd make sure she was busy every single day!

''Ask your boss for more time one day. It can't hurt. I'm sure your aunt would like to show off Kinsinger Electronics.''

''Mmm.'' She was almost finished. Glancing at his plate, she almost groaned. He had over half his meal left. Was there any way to encourage him to eat faster?

Dodging pitfalls for potential exposure during the rest of the meal, Karla was relieved when Matt finally called for the check. She alternated between being fascinated with their conversation, and scared silly she'd say something stupid and blow her cover.

When they walked out of the restaurant, she smiled and held out her hand.

''Thanks for dinner. And this afternoon. I hope you enjoyed seeing Stanley Park.''

He took her hand and tucked it in the crook of his arm, not shaking it goodbye like she wanted.

"I'm taking you home. We'll get a cab." He looked down the street.

"Actually, I don't live too far away, I can walk."

Raising one eyebrow, he shrugged. "If you like, but it's colder than earlier. I think a cab would be better."

"I can get home by myself."

"Is there a reason you don't want me taking you to your apartment? I didn't plan to invite myself in. What with you having to do your hair and all."

Karla bit her bottom lip. He was teasing her. She almost giggled. It did sound stupid. But she was afraid he'd remember the address that had been on her résumé.

"No reason at all," she said faintly. None she could give him.

He hailed a cab and in less time than she wanted, they pulled to a stop in front of her apartment building.

Matt climbed out and held the door for her. She didn't see any evidence of suspicion. He asked the driver to wait, which Karla took as a good sign, then went with her into the building.

Arriving on her floor, he walked her to the door of her flat.

"Thanks again," she said, fishing out her keys. "I had a great time." Inserting them in the lock, she opened the door and turned back one last time.

Matt was right there. He put his hands on her shoulders and leaned closer to brush his lips against hers. "Thanks for going out on such short notice, friend."

She nodded, incapable of speech. She thought her brain circuits had just been fried. Touching the tip of her tongue lightly to her lips, she imagined she could taste him.

With a soft groan, Matt pulled her into his arms and kissed her again. This was no brush of lips, but a full lips-moving-against-lips, tongue-tracing-the-seam, plunging-in-for-a-taste kiss.

Karla wrapped her arms around him and held on, thrilled with the excitement that exploded. His mouth was warm and electrifying, giving new meaning to the term kissed. His arms were strong, yet held her gently, sensually. His body was hard, pressing against her, making her conscious of her own softer curves and femininity.

When he broke the kiss, it was all she could do to remain upright. She'd never suffered from wobbly knees before meeting Matt Gramling. Now it seemed it was a regular occurrence. She was vaguely pleased to notice he was breathing as hard as she was. At least it hadn't been all one-sided.

"If you don't call by Tuesday, I'll call you," he said. Then he turned and headed for the elevator.

Karla watched until the doors slid closed behind him, then entered the flat. It was too bad he'd sworn off marriage—he needed to be locked up to protect the rest of womankind!

"Good grief," she said. "I'm in big trouble here." Dashing to the front window, she leaned her forehead against it to see the cab on the street below. In only seconds, Matt came out and climbed in.

"Don't go acting like some love-struck teenager," she murmured, watching as the cab drove away. "There is definitely no future in it!" Matt had made that clear.

But for a second, Karla thought it might be too late for such sage advice.

Turning from the window, she tried to come up with a way to refuse lunch without making an issue about it.

One of the things Matt Gramling had always prided himself on was the ability to compartmentalize his life. There was work. Business consumed most of his waking hours. He liked it that way. The challenges and problems to be dealt with gave him an outlet to be creative and innovative. The successful solutions gave satisfaction. Knowing he was building for the future, expanding and making a difference in the lives of hundreds of employees was fulfilling.

Of course when he took his wilderness trips, he closed off the business end and focused on nature, on the feel of the land, of the challenges living off the earth afforded. On the contentment he felt at the end of each day, falling asleep by a fire, knowing once more he'd pitted himself against the elements and won.

Rarely did he need to compartmentalize relationships. He dated casually, enjoying the company of women. Sometimes even developing an intimate aspect that lasted for months on end. But when apart, he had other things to think about.

Until this morning.

He threw down his pen and rose, walking to the window with the view of Coal Harbour and Vancouver's North Shore. He didn't see it, however. Before him danced an image of Karla Jones. He remembered her funny comments. Heard her laugh. Almost felt her in his arms again.

Had he been too long between women? Winding up his day-to-day involvement in the Toronto firm had been grueling. And plunging into Kinsinger Electronics, with a self-imposed mandate to turn it around as quickly as he could, was equally consuming. He hadn't had a date in months since the one planned for last Friday had not panned out.

Until yesterday.

He'd been up-front and clear with Karla. He wasn't looking for a long-term relationship. Fortunately, neither was she. That's just how he liked things.

While they had hit it off, she had not seemed excited for a second date. In fact, he had the feeling she was stalling. Deliberately not accepting a date in any way shape or form. Had he misread the signs?

Hearing a noise in the outer office, Matt turned and crossed to the opened door. Jeannette straightened after putting away her purse.

For a moment, he was able to observe her without her being aware of his presence. The resemblance between Karla and Jeannette was strong, but as he studied her, he could see the differences. Jeannette was a bit heavier, as was common with women in their fifties. And her hair was long, gray, pulled back into a tidy, neat bun, with never a strand out of place.

Karla's dark, glossy hair had danced in the wind yesterday.

"Good morning."

She looked up, startled. Then nodded gravely. "Good morning, Mr. Gramling."

He almost smiled. She persisted in holding to formality.

"I met your niece this weekend." He didn't need to tell her. But unless Karla had called her aunt after he left her at her flat, Jeannette wouldn't know. And for some reason, he wanted her to know.

"Karla?" she asked.

He nodded. "We went to dinner last night."

"Oh." She remained silent.

"Is there a problem?"

Shaking her head, she picked up a pad and two pencils. "No problem," she said.

One day he would find out something that was a problem for her. But thankfully his dating her niece wasn't one.

CHAPTER FOUR

EACH morning, Matt liked to meet with Jeannette first thing to prioritize tasks for the day. And to touch base. Then he let her get on with her own work. He liked that time before the frenetic pace of the day took hold. It had been his practice for years. Meeting with Jeannette was different from his morning briefings with Sara in Toronto, however.

Jeannette brought something more to the meetings. A fresh way of looking at things. A willingness to voice her opinions. And a sense of serenity that was oddly appealing to a man who thrived on the fast pace of business.

Once they were seated in his office, he reviewed the reports he'd read that weekend at the cabin—several needed more in-depth analysis from the managers and he directed her to obtain them. Two deserved special praise for being so complete and he asked her to draft a note to that effect in his name.

He glanced up and found Jeannette's gaze on his mouth. For a second he was startled.

She met his gaze and promptly dropped her own to the tablet. A hint of color stained her cheeks.

For an awkward moment, Matt felt nonplussed. Was she wondering if he'd kissed her niece? The memory of those kisses burned into his mind. He could still feel the effects twelve hours later and half a city away.

He glanced at Jeannette's mouth. There was a faint

sheen as if she wore some kind of lip gloss, but it wasn't the bright red lipstick Karla had worn. And her lips were tightened—with disapproval?

Hell, maybe it was going to be a problem dating her niece after all.

"You mentioned on Friday that you wanted me to set up a meeting with the Percell Group this week. I couldn't reach Richard Taylor on Friday, so will continue to try this morning," Jeannette said primly.

Matt tossed one of the reports across the desk. "That's the report by Myers about the Percell Group. Apparently they were one of our biggest customers a year or so ago. We dropped the ball and they went elsewhere. I want to get them back. You might want to read the report. I think this is a deal that with the right touch, will bring a major turnaround in the company. A lot of bang for the buck."

"You still want an initial lunch meeting?"

"Yes."

"Why?"

He looked up. "What?"

"I'm just wondering why you'd want a lunch meeting instead of meeting here where you'd be able to get facts and figures at the touch of a finger. At lunch, you'll be winging it."

He nodded. "This is the preliminary round. I want to meet the decision-makers. See what they are like. Find out what they want, then tailor a presentation to match their needs."

She looked thoughtful. "So you're not just selling them on how great we are now."

"We aren't great right now. It'll take time to turn the company around. And one way to do it is make sure we give the customer exactly what he wants. But we need to find that out, not assume we can make that determination based on what we think he should want.''

''So maybe I should do a bit more background work, myself,'' she murmured.

''In what way?''

''I could ask Mr. Taylor's secretary what his likes and dislikes are. Get a feel from that perspective.''

He nodded. ''Good idea. But don't push it if she's reluctant.''

''I'll be the soul of discretion.''

''I know I can count on you, Jeannette.'' He hesitated a moment, then added, ''Include yourself in for lunch. If you're going to be my right hand, might as well see this project through from the beginning. I want input from you, as well, if you see something I've missed. Or the managers haven't thought about.''

Not for the first time Karla wondered if what she was doing would end up in a total disaster. The ideal job, and she was playing fast and loose with her boss. For the first time she gave serious thought to coming clean with everything before he was convinced of her abilities.

It was after nine by the time Karla returned to her desk. Matt had reviewed plans and requested meetings and scheduled conference calls for the rest of the day. He'd also asked her to draft responses to most of the mail he'd received.

Even with a full day's work ahead, she almost danced to her desk. She loved the responsibility he gave her, relished the challenge.

After only a week, he was loading her up with important tasks, utilizing her skills and experience—and her own innate sense of business which she'd garnered under Mr. Daniels's tutelage. And already talking as if she was his right hand! She was going to show him how competent a twenty-eight-year-old could be.

In the center of her desk lay an envelope addressed in printed letters to *Miss Jones*. Placing the folders and correspondence from Matt's office down, she picked up the envelope and opened it.

A single typewritten sheet was inside with a very brief missive.

I know who you are. Don't you think Matt Gramling would find it interesting?

Karla sank onto her chair, rereading the words in stunned disbelief.

She rose and went to peer into the reception area, but the hallway was empty all the way to the elevator. Glancing over her shoulder, she was relieved to see Matt had not followed her to ask what she was doing. Who could have put the note on her desk? And why?

Folding the sheet, she slipped it into its envelope and slid it into her purse. What did it mean? Was someone planning to blow the whistle on her?

She definitely needed to speed up her schedule to let Matt know her age.

She took a deep breath and reached out to sort the work in front of her. Not yet, though. She still had to show she was indispensable before risking his knowing who she really was. Or rather, how old she really was.

Who could have sent the note? Briefly she toyed with various managers she'd met over the last week. Somehow it didn't seem like it could be any of them.

It took effort, but Karla gradually pushed away her

curiosity about the note and plunged into the work piled on her desk. She'd have to worry about that later, she had things to do.

She called Mr. Taylor's secretary at the Percell Group and forthrightly explained what she was interested in learning. After ascertaining his preferences, she asked to be connected to arrange a lunch meeting.

He'd been gracious on the phone, agreeing to a Thursday lunch. His wife would accompany him, he said. Karla knew that from the secretary's information. While not divulging anything of a confidential nature, the woman had told her she often thought Mrs. Taylor was the driving force behind the company.

After spending Sunday afternoon together, it proved harder than Karla had expected to ignore Matt during the workday. She could hear the murmur of his voice through the open door when he spoke on the phone. And she'd remembered his voice at dinner. She heard his laughter once, and her heart skipped a beat. She wished she could see his face. She knew she'd be mesmerized.

As when he'd been reviewing the day's schedule earlier, she'd practically been mesmerized by his mouth. Those lips had kissed her like she'd never been kissed before. For a moment she grew dreamy just remembering.

His catching her staring had embarrassed her, but the warmth from the memory of those kisses remained. She found herself anticipating briefing him on the Percell Group lunch plans—just to see him again.

She stepped in his office before lunch.

When she told him of the confirmed luncheon date, he jotted the appointment in his personal calendar. ''Good work. I like the fact we'll be taking him to his favorite restaurant. That was a good idea to question the secretary.''

She nodded, reluctant to leave.

He looked at her for a moment. ''What would you do if someone called you to ask you the same thing?''

''Tell them what was available for public knowledge— to foster a feeling of cooperation. Unfortunately, I don't yet know which restaurant is your favorite here in Vancouver.''

''I'll have to try several, I can see. I invited your niece to lunch one day this week. I hope you'll join us. Maybe you or she can suggest a place I would enjoy.''

''I can call her if you like.'' Karla had a brilliant idea—she'd pretend to call herself and tell Matt the only day she could make lunch was Thursday. For a long-term solution, it only bought her a little time. But better than being put on the spot. If she had any sense at all she'd forget seeing Matt socially.

But common sense seemed in short supply today. Despite the pitfalls of last evening, she wanted to spend time with him. Wanted to see him away from the office. Maybe share another kiss or two?

She knew she should just tell him as Karla she wasn't interested. But there was no way she could lie that much. There was something very alluring about Matt Gramling. And the truth was she did want to see him again. He'd said he wanted to be friends. She could test the waters— see how it went.

The image of that note on her desk flashed into mind. For one crazy moment she almost considered confiding in him the next time she saw him as Karla. What did the sender plan to accomplish?

By the end of the day, Karla was having second, third and fourth thoughts about her brilliant plan. She loved her new job, relished working with Matt, but the strain of the whole scheme was beginning to wear. Especially with the threat of the letter writer hanging over her.

She'd told Matt in the late afternoon that Karla couldn't make lunch. He'd nodded and moved on to other topics. She couldn't tell if he were disappointed or not. Maybe he was only following up because he'd said he would and it really didn't matter one way or another. The thought left her a bit disappointed.

Karla had just stepped out of her bathroom where she'd scrubbed her face clean of all the heavy makeup a couple of hours later when her cell phone rang. Dashing into the living room, she scrambled through her purse to find it, flipping it open.

"Hello?" she said breathlessly.

"Busy all week?" Matt's familiar voice said.

"Uh, actually I had Thursday free, but I understand you're busy that day."

"Next week?"

So much for it not mattering. A warm glow settled in the region of her heart. She sat on the sofa and pulled her feet up, feeling free and excited. He hadn't let on in front of Jeannette, but he had wanted to see her!

"Why do you always ask when I'm not near my calendar?"

"Why didn't you anticipate I would ask and check your calendar before leaving work today?" he countered.

"I guess I didn't think you'd follow up," she said slowly.

"Why not? I thought you'd like to see where your aunt works."

"I'll make sure I swing by someday."

"Make sure you do it when I'm free. I want to show the place to you myself."

"Oh."

"Sure, so I can get your comment directly. I know I can trust a friend to speak the truth, right?"

"Oh, right."

"How did your busy day go? Eat lunch on the fly?"

"Something like that. It was hectic, but I love my job. And I didn't have to work overtime tonight."

Oops, would he associate that with his own executive assistant leaving on time today?

"Do you have to work overtime much?"

"Only as assignments warrant. And I don't mind. I want to be viewed as a team player."

"Your aunt said something like that last week. It's gratifying from an employer's point of view. And unusual in someone so young."

"Me?" she asked.

"I find older workers usually have a stronger work ethic and don't mind doing whatever is needed to get the job done. Younger workers are more self-centered and interested in doing what is best for them, not the company."

"I don't think that's an age assessment. It's more an individual thing," Karla countered, annoyed with his statement.

"In your vast experience?"

"Well, I have worked a number of years in the real world and have seen both young and old goofing off, and young and old putting out one-hundred-ten percent! Age had nothing to do with it. What do you plan to do, fire everyone under a certain age at Kinsinger and only hire older workers?"

"No, but I made sure my own personal assistant was more mature. No flighty young woman who is more interested in flirting than working."

"That's an unfair assessment. A lot of young employees work hard! You're saying you wouldn't even give a younger woman a chance to work for you?"

Ever? Maybe she would be stuck pretending to be twenty-some years older for her entire career. The thought had her close her eyes in frustration.

"It's a moot point, don't you think, Karla? Your aunt is settling in nicely. I won't have to look for anyone else, young or old."

"And what if she gets swept away with romance, gets married and leaves?"

"Do you think it's likely?"

She was silent a moment. "No." The only one she could imagine sweeping her away right now was her boss, and as far as he knew, she was twenty years older than he.

Maybe Pat had been right, it had been a dumb idea. One she was stuck with if she wanted to keep her job.

"Of all the things we could talk about, why discuss abstract theories about age and work ethic?"

"If my aunt left, would you hire me?"

The silence lasted several seconds. "Your aunt isn't leaving."

"But if she did and I applied for the job would you hire me? I've got good skills. I'm not flighty. And I could bring excellent references."

"No, I don't think I would," he said slowly.

"Gee, thanks a bunch."

"Probably not for the reasons you're thinking."

"How do you know what I'm thinking?"

"I wouldn't hire you because of the attraction between us," he said, ignoring her last comment.

Karla felt heat wash through her. That was blunt. Then it turned to a warm glow. The attraction wasn't all one-sided! Of course, she hoped for that after his searing kisses.

"I thought it was just me."

"Lady, you about set the world on fire just walking down the sidewalk. A man would have to be half dead not to notice. But I have definite rules against seeing staff members socially. So, no, I wouldn't hire you."

"Oh."

"But since you don't work for me, I have no rules against seeing you again."

"How nice for me," she said, that familiar bumping in her heart starting up again. Would she ever get used to it?

"So if lunch is out, how about dinner one night this week?"

"During the week?" she stalled, trying desperately to think of a reason to refuse. She wouldn't put it past him to invite himself over for that home-cooked meal he talked about.

"I want to see you again and I can't make it next weekend. I'm going up to the cabin again. In fact, I'm planning to ask your aunt if she can accompany me. We're working on a new proposal for a former client and I want to get it nailed down as quickly as possible. We can get a lot more accomplished away from distractions.''

A weekend at that remote cabin—just her and Matt? She'd better start thinking up excuses fast. There was no way she could pull off being the mature woman he thought her for an entire weekend. She had to wash that makeup off after a few hours to give her skin time to breathe. And she couldn't sleep in that itchy wig. Just her luck they'd have a fire or something and she'd run outside au naturel and he'd know instantly—

''Karla?''

''Huh? Oh, sorry. No, this week's not convenient for dinner.''

''Busy every night?''

''Usually I don't go out on dates during the week.''

''No date, just dinner with a friend.''

Oh, right, he wanted to be *friends*. Could she even entertain that idea? Somehow he and Kevin didn't fit in the same category.

''Come on, we both have to eat. How about we find a nice place, have a quiet dinner, and I'll have you home before ten.''

She laughed. ''You make me sound like I'm in high school.''

''You can't be long out.''

He *did* think she was younger than she was! She opened her mouth to tell him she'd been supporting herself for eight years, then snapped it shut. Good grief, she couldn't confess to matching her aunt's work record. He'd catch on instantly.

"Longer than you think."

"You can tell me over dinner."

She blew out a gust of air, her bangs flying every which way. "Sheesh, you're persistent. All right. How about Wednesday?"

"Shall we go out, or have dinner at your place?"

"I thought you were taking me out."

"I remembered the offer of a home-cooked meal."

"I never offered!"

"Mmm, I could have sworn—"

"Okay, fine! Dinner here. But not until seven." And heaven help her if she had to stay late at work that night!

"So what'll you cook?" he asked.

"Maybe I'll get take-out."

"I was looking forward to a home-cooked meal."

"People who invite themselves over can't be choosy."

"Damn! I was already anticipating something from an old family recipe."

She felt her bones melting. That sexy voice did funny things to her insides. If he continued along those lines, she'd promise him anything.

"Okay, pasta. How's that? With my grandmother's sauce, and French bread and salad."

"I'll bring some wine."

Had that been the only reason he'd called? Karla didn't want him to ring off. Wishing to keep him on the line, she came up with the first topic she could think of, "Tell me about your cabin. Will my aunt like it?"

"It's a bit rustic—log construction, but big and roomy. It's right on the water, so getting there and back is easy with the plane. And I have an office set up in one of the ground-floor rooms that almost matches the one at Kinsinger with equipment and communications capability.''

''Mmm.''

''And that means?''

''I'd think if you have a rustic cabin for a retreat from the stress and hectic schedule of work, the last thing you'd want was to be working.''

''Ah, but this is a work retreat. When I really want to escape, I head for the wilderness.''

''So tell me more about your wilderness adventures,'' she invited, settling back and closing her eyes. Listening to him talk to her about his last camping trip, she could envision the wild country he tackled. She wished she could see him tramping through the forest, building fires to cook and for warmth, fending for himself in the wilderness. But it didn't sound like her cup of tea. Listening was better.

Sometime later she realized they'd been on the phone almost an hour. The time had flown.

''I have to go,'' she said reluctantly. It was getting late, and she still needed to eat dinner before bedtime.

''I'll see you Wednesday.''

She hung up, wondering if he would call between now and their dinner date. She wouldn't mind talking to him again before then.

Of course she would, she thought with a giggle. She'd see him tomorrow morning at eight!

By the next morning, Karla was a nervous wreck. First she had not come up with a convincing excuse to avoid a weekend trip with Matt. Second, she was having mis-

74 HIS SECRETARY'S SECRET

givings about his coming to dinner. How could she concentrate on work with so much else going on?

Promptly at seven Wednesday evening the bell to her apartment rang. Karla took a deep breath and went to answer it. She'd put on dark leggings and a bright blue silk top. Makeup on, cheeks smooth and unblemished, and her hair a silky dark cap, she was as ready as she was going to be. Butterflies danced in her stomach. She knew she was flirting with discovery. She swallowed hard, pasted on a bright smile and flung open the door.

"Prompt, I see," she said in greeting, her eyes going wide.

He looked wonderful! He'd changed since work. The charcoal-gray slacks were crisp, the white shirt, open at the throat, threw his tan into dark relief. The sports jacket emphasized his broad shoulders. And the smile that greeted her had her knees wobbling again. She hoped she wasn't drooling, but her mind seemed turned to mush. How could he look so different from the stern employer? A brief change of clothes wrought miracles.

He handed her a wrapped bottle of wine. "I said I'd bring the wine. You look lovely."

"Thank you."

He looked into the apartment, then back to Karla, waiting.

"Oh, come in." She stepped aside, wanting to smack her hand against her head. He'd think she was totally insane.

Glancing around, he waited as she shut the door. "This suits you. I wondered if you'd have lots of modern things. The country look is surprising, yet warm and inviting."

"Come in the kitchen while I finish fixing dinner. You can tell me all about your day."

He soon opened the wine and poured them each a glass, then leaned against the counter—much too close for comfort, Karla thought, wondering if having him in the kitchen was such a good idea.

She sipped her wine, then returned to cutting the fresh vegetables for the salad. The pesto sauce had been made, and the water was almost ready for the pasta.

"I'd rather you tell me about your day," he said.

She looked at him, caught by the intensity of his eyes. "It was fine."

"Do you realize how reticent you are about your life?" he asked curiously.

"I'm not, I'm an open book."

"So tell me something you did today."

Stalling, hoping for inspiration, Karla turned back to the vegetables, dumping them into the large salad bowl. "My best friend had a baby today. She called and left word on my answering machine."

Pat had left a long message explaining that she'd wanted to call Karla at work, but hadn't dared. When Karla had returned the call, they'd spent thirty minutes excitedly discussing her new baby girl. Karla made plans to visit Friday evening—Pat and baby Brittany would be home by then.

She glanced at him and grinned. "Probably not something you want to talk about a lot, is it? Not being interested in marriage and all. But my friend and her husband are crazy about each other and thrilled to death with the birth of their first child."

"Someone has to perpetuate the species."

She laughed. "Confess, you're not as hard-hearted as you like to make out. Don't you like babies?"

"I've never been around them."

"Me, either. At least not a lot. But the few I've seen are precious."

"And does that make your own biological clock start ticking?" he asked.

She shook her head. "You have a narrow view of women. We do not spend every waking moment worrying about a biological clock!"

His eyes danced in amusement as he reached out to brush an errant strand of hair back. She drew in her breath. His touch was electrifying.

Matt let his fingers toy with her hair. It was as soft as silk. He heard her sharp intake and almost smiled, liking the fact she grew flustered. She had a similar effect on him, it was only fair to reciprocate.

His finger trailed along her cheek. Her skin was smooth and lightly flushed. She was lovely. And, thanks to her aunt, he knew exactly how she'd look when she was twenty or thirty years older.

The thought surprised him. Dropping his hand, he leaned back against the counter and studied her. He had never once thought about another woman twenty or thirty years ahead. Had she cast some kind of spell? He was not looking for long-term commitment. A few dates, some good times together, then they'd part and he'd find another companion.

He certainly wouldn't be around twenty years from now to care about how Karla had aged.

She turned and opened the utensil drawer. "Home-

cooked meals come with strings. Here—'' She brought
out forks and knives and handed them to him. ''You can
set the table while I throw the pasta in the water. It'll be
ready soon and is best served hot and fresh.''

He took the utensils and headed for the table he'd seen
in the alcove off the living room, glad to have something
to do to take his mind off the disturbing thoughts of a
future with Karla. He had his life just as he wanted it.
And a complication with a woman wasn't in his plans.

He set the table, then checked out the view from her
window. Not very inspiring, just other buildings, and a
glimpse of the sky. Though at night he expected it was
pretty with all the lights on.

When he found a permanent place, he wanted a view
of the bay. For a moment he let his imagination envisiage
a spacious flat with a panoramic view. He'd decorate it
in country comfort and make it as warm and welcoming
at the end of the day as Karla's flat was.

He jerked away from the window and the foolish daydreams. He wasn't into country charm. He liked sleek,
modern lines. Glass and chrome and leather. Glancing
around, however, he couldn't help contrasting his place
in Toronto with Karla's. He refused to admit hers had his
beat as a place to wind down in.

Anyway, he was usually caught up with work. He
didn't spend a lot of time at home—unless it was also
working.

But would he, an insidious voice inside asked, if it was
as welcoming as Karla's place? If Karla was there each
evening to give him a choice between work and pleasure?

Now he was losing it.

She came into the room, carrying a bowl of bright

spring flowers. Placing it in the center of the small table, she tilted her head as she studied the effect. She smiled serenely up at him.

"I love flowers, don't you? I got these from a street vendor. I think they brighten up the place."

"You make it bright," he said slowly, reaching out to draw her into his arms. Time to worry about his careening thoughts later. Right now he wanted to kiss her.

CHAPTER FIVE

IT WAS as if she had been waiting for his kiss. Her body aligned perfectly with his. Her arms were warm and strong around his shoulders and neck. Her mouth seemed to be made for his.

Deepening the kiss, Matt relished the excitement holding her brought. His body hummed with energy and desire. Drawing her even closer, deepening the kiss, he wondered how long it would be before he could take her to bed. He knew she'd be explosive—look how responsive she was to a mere kiss.

Not that the embrace could be classified as a mere anything. He'd always scoffed at the romantic notion some people had given to desire. But there was something soft and almost sweet about the hot passion that sprang between them. Some of it had to be due to her own air of innocence—impossible though it was.

Vaguely he was aware of a dinging noise.

"Oops." Karla pulled back. "The pasta."

She turned and hurried into the kitchen, while Matt tried to get his rollicking emotions under control. The way he felt right now, they could skip dinner and head straight for dessert!

Waiting until things were under control, he followed her into the kitchen. Karla heaped pasta on their plates, concentrating on her task as if it were the most crucial aspect in world peace.

He leaned over and brushed his lips against the nape of her neck, revealed when she leaned forward. Her short hair was sexy. He thought he liked long hair on women, but that tantalizing exposure of her neck affected him as nothing else ever had.

"It's ready," she said brightly.

Recognizing temporary defeat when he saw it, he nodded and gave up on the kisses—for now.

"Want some more wine?"

"Yes, please." She sounded breathless. The surge of satisfaction that swept through him was astonishing. He always liked to please the women he was with, but with Karla it went deeper. He wanted to be the only one to please her, and satisfy her. To find out what she liked, and show her he could fulfill all her needs.

He wanted to find out more about her. What her favorite movie was, and did she have a crush on some movie star. Did she like to read, or listen to music? What was her preferred way to spend a Saturday afternoon?

Dinner was not awkward as he feared it might be after their kiss. She was more open and forthcoming than at any time since he'd met her. Asking the questions he wanted most to know about, he found out about movies she liked, about her family holidays at Okanagan Lake, about the mystery books she loved and the soft jazz she listened to. He was pleased to note she liked action adventure movies and there was no crush! Her love of romance novels threw him. But she teased him by saying she knew he wouldn't enjoy them—they contained the L-and C-words—love and commitment.

Once again Matt felt at home with a woman he'd recently met. Her demeanor reminded him of how he felt around her aunt. There was something about the Jones women that put men at ease. Maybe it was knowing neither saw him as husband material.

"Your turn," she said. "I've been talking almost nonstop. Tell me what your favorite subject was at the university."

He hesitated a moment, then nodded. It wasn't something anyone else had ever asked. "English lit."

She blinked. "Really? I would never have suspected it. I thought for sure you'd like something like Corporate Raiders 101."

"I took an English literature course each year. Initially to fulfill a basic requirement. But I found reading the classics a welcomed break from the analytical and mathematical emphasis of the business courses. And a way to get caught up in the action of a time and place so different from the one in which we live."

"You're a romantic," she said slowly, her smile breaking through. "A closet one, I hasten to add."

He shook his head, amused by her teasing.

"I bet you envisioned yourself as Sidney Carlton, saving a friend. Or Tom Jones, out for a rollicking time."

"I fancied myself the Scarlet Pimpernel," he reluctantly admitted.

"*That* was included in the syllabus? Your professor was also a romantic."

"Extra credit, and a great adventure."

She studied him through narrowed eyes. "Yes, I can see you as the Scarlet Pimpernel, swashbuckling and ready for adventure—risking life and limb for a cause."

"Maybe not that far."

"Of course you'd go that far. Don't you risk life and limb on your trips to the wilderness?"

He shook his head.

"What happens if you get sick, or attacked by a bear? You're miles from help, from human contact. You could be killed and no one would ever know what happened to you."

"There's no one to care what happens to me," he said gently.

Karla's eyes grew wide. He saw the realization hit, and then the softening as compassion filled her.

"I'd care," she said softly.

He felt the words like a kick in the gut. He'd been on his own for so long, he never thought to hear someone say that.

"I make sure I always come back."

"As the Scarlet Pimpernel always did. But don't forget, he had the help of a good woman at the end."

"So you'll come rescue me?"

Karla laughed. "Not unless you're tangled up somewhere in Stanley Park. That's about as wild as I go."

"You'll have to expand your horizons. Maybe spend a weekend with me at Henley Island. We can practice wilderness lifesaving tips there. Among other things," he said suggestively.

He was charmed by the wave of color that swept into her cheeks. She couldn't possibly be as naive as she sometimes acted. No modern woman living in such a cosmopolitan city as Vancouver could have remained innocent approaching her mid twenties. But it didn't matter. He, himself, wasn't without experience, why should he expect a partner to be?

But for one crazy moment, he almost wished she were as innocent as she appeared.

His comment threw her. Karla knew what going off for a weekend with a man entailed. Was he serious? Was she ready to take such a step? She loved spending time with Matt—whether at work or on their off hours. But she hadn't known him long. And it would comprise a huge step for her.

Still, imagine the two of them, with nothing to do but get to know each other better, and enjoy the outdoors. It was something she'd have to consider carefully. She didn't want to get hurt, or plunge foolishly into something beyond her control.

"Does going to Henley mean campfire cooking?"

"The cabin has a kitchen."

"And who cooks?"

"After this meal, I'd say you do. This is delicious."

"I'm happy you like it, but—" she wrinkled her nose "—I'm not sure my repertoire of meals would last a weekend." She was pleased when he asked for seconds on the pasta and sauce. He really did enjoy it.

"You don't cook dinner each night?"

She shook her head. "For one it's not worth it."

"But there would be two of us at the cabin."

She reached for her wine, took a sip. "Then no reason we can't share the responsibility, is there?" she asked.

"My experience is probably more limited than yours."

"Then there'll be things I can teach you, won't there?" She held his gaze, feeling reckless.

Matt laughed aloud. Karla smiled brightly, delighting

in the way the conversation sparkled. She wished for more evenings like tonight.

And if she got her wish, she'd have to decide how far to take this relationship—in light of Mr. 25-50's rule, and marriage phobia.

And in light of her masquerade at work. The thought threw a damper on the evening. Some of the zest vanished.

"Dessert?" she asked, rising to clear the table.

"Depends on what you have in mind."

He was doing it deliberately, she knew. He was so different from anyone she'd ever dated before. His sexy flirting keep her constantly on her toes. And she loved every moment.

"Chocolate mousse," she said, rising and reaching for his plate.

His hand caught her wrist, holding her loosely. "What if I want something different?"

Her heart caught in her throat. "I have some brandy?" She knew what he meant, and it had nothing to do with brandy.

His thumb caressed the soft skin of her wrist. She almost dropped the plate. Surely he could hear her heart pounding. The blood rushing through her veins sounded like a waterfall. Her gaze locked with his. She recognized desire—wondering if he saw a like expression reflected in hers.

Dropping her gaze to his mouth, she wanted to release the plates, drop on his lap and kiss him senseless. Or at least until one of them was senseless. And it probably wouldn't be him.

A hint of caution had her hesitate. There was something about Matt's never losing control that jarred. She was the one who seemed to lose control when he kissed her.

But what a glorious loss!

"Don't you like chocolate mousse?" she asked.

His hand tightened slightly, then released her. Rising, he took his own plate. "I like mousse."

"Sit still. I'll clear and get dessert."

"Just showing you how well things will work if we go to the cabin. Though my dessert might be different," he said suggestively.

She knew exactly what kind of dessert he had in mind.

By the time they'd had mousse, coffee and a small snifter of brandy in the living room, Karla's nerves were ragged. She knew she was toying with danger, but was fascinated—as a moth was to flame.

Everything about Matt was riveting—from the way his eyes crinkled when he smiled, to the strength of his muscles when he held her, to the wry sense of humor he rarely showed. Time had flown by and it was getting late, but she didn't want the evening to end.

If she had a lick of sense, she'd send Matt on his way and never see him again outside of the office. But she couldn't resist the lure of spending more time with him. If he asked her out again, she'd throw caution to the wind and accept. She never suspected she had this hidden flare for danger.

He checked his watch. "It's getting late—for a work night anyway. I'll be on my way."

Karla felt disappointed.

"I've enjoyed tonight, Karla. Thanks for inviting me. I wouldn't say no to another invitation. In the meantime,

I'll tender one officially. Next Wednesday evening? We could find a restaurant that has music, maybe dancing. I'd make it this weekend, but I'll need to work on the deal we're trying to consummate,'' Matt said as they walked together to the door.

"I'll check my calendar and let you know," she temporized. Next Wednesday? A lifetime away. Yet was she ready for another evening with Matt? At least in a neutral place like a restaurant, she would be better able to keep a rein on temptation.

He touched her cheek when they stopped by the door.

"I'm going to get you a pocket calendar so you can carry it with you at all times. If you do have something going on, it can't be that exciting that you can't remember it."

"I don't usually date during the week. I'm a working gal, you know," she retorted honestly.

"Then we won't stay out late. Come to dinner with me."

He put his hands gently on her shoulders, pulling her into an embrace. Lowering his head, he kissed with the passion that had been simmering all evening.

Karla let go of her inhibitions and returned the kiss with all the fervor in her. When in his arms, she didn't think. If he asked her now, she'd agree to anything as long as it included him!

"We're two adults who are attracted to each other. And who have no other commitments. We're not looking for forever. Dinner between friends. Maybe a dance or two. I'd like to hold you and sway to music. Say you'll come," he mumbled against her lips.

For a vague instant she rather thought she wanted commitment and a future together. But he was talking dinner. And a chance to spend more time with him. How could she refuse?

"I'll call you," he said, straightening. "Thanks again for dinner."

He cupped her neck and brushed his lips across hers again then turned and headed down the hall.

She watched as he strode to the elevator. Once the doors slid closed behind him, she turned and slowly reentered her flat. Sighing as she closed the door. She wished she knew what to do about the disturbingly masculine male who just left. And the raging hormones that engulfed her whenever he was near.

He'd made it abundantly clear he was not looking for any long-range relationship. But she wondered if her friend Pat had been correct—when Mr. Right came along, all her own protestations about wanting a career over marriage went out the window.

Mr. Right? Matt Gramling? She shook her head. When she fell in love, she wanted it to be with some man who would adore her in return. Not Mr. Burned-Once-And-Never-Committing-Again.

But as she washed the dishes and put them away, she wondered if she wasn't already a little too late in her caution. She was very much afraid she was falling head over heels for the man.

Time to put on the brakes.

No dancing. Dinner wouldn't be so bad—but definitely no dancing!

Late Thursday morning, Karla began to wonder if she'd imagined his saying he was inviting her aunt to the weekend retreat to work. He'd made no mention of it that morning. Did he expect to spring it on her as she was leaving on Friday afternoon?

She had dressed carefully that morning, in anticipation of lunch with Mr. and Mrs. Taylor. Her position at Kinsinger Electronics kept her isolated from the majority of the other clerical workers, so she hadn't worried too much about another woman seeing through her disguise.

But Mrs. Taylor would be spending a couple of hours with her in a close setting. Would the woman see through the makeup and question why she was pretending?

As the lunch hour drew closer, Karla wondered if she should plead a headache or something and excuse herself from joining them. She couldn't risk exposure—especially in front of a major prospective client.

Yet, she couldn't bring herself to back out and leave Matt in the lurch. She was a professional. If Mrs. Taylor showed signs of noticing something was wrong, maybe she could quietly explain and hope for her silence.

Sheesh, another dumb idea, she thought as she reviewed the notes she'd taken from the Percell Group report. She should be trying to promote the company, not discussing her own situation. It would make Matt look bad—that he hadn't recognized a masquerade when he saw one. And she would do nothing to jeopardize his relationship with these prospective clients.

Crossing her fingers for luck, Karla went to brazen it out.

She was looking forward to seeing Matt in action. She knew from his history he was good at turning things around. Today she'd see exactly how he did it.

She had to remind herself to focus on business. Twice during their briefing that morning, she'd caught herself gazing at him, remembering their kisses, their lively conversation from the night before. Fortunately, she'd glanced down at her notes before he'd discovered his staid, mature Miss Jones mooning over him. She gave herself a stern talking-to. She had to remain totally professional and forget about his arms holding her, his fingers brushing lightly against her cheek. His mouth devouring hers and leaving her breathless.

The Taylors were an older couple, already at the restaurant when Matt and Karla arrived. Introductions were made and they all were soon seated at a private table with a view of the city spread before them. The lighting was favorable, and Karla breathed a sigh of relief. Hopefully her makeup would bear up to scrutiny.

"So you've taken over Kinsinger Electronics, eh, young man?" Richard Taylor said heartily once their beverage orders had been taken.

"Now, dear, of course he has," his wife said, perusing the menu.

"Taken over, taken charge and moving it in a new direction. One I think you might be interested in helping me forge," Matt said easily.

"What? How could I help?"

"I'd like some insight into what went wrong when we had your account. And what you would have liked to have seen? What could the company have done to keep your business? One thing I don't want to do is repeat the past. We all know where that got Kinsinger."

"Very good plan," Mrs. Taylor said, joining the conversation. "So many times one's firm changes and its suppliers or customers can't keep up."

"And Mr. Moore was a bit old-fashioned," Matt said.

Mrs. Taylor looked at Karla, her gaze friendly. "And how do you fit into all this?"

"I'm Mr. Gramling's executive assistant," she said quietly.

"Ah." Mrs. Taylor smiled. "Then tell me something about his management style."

Karla looked at Matt. When he gave an almost imperceptible nod, she felt free to talk. "I find it open and aboveboard. I've just started working with him, but from what I can see, he takes time to gather information from which to make decisions—whether personnel related, customer relations, or from his management team. And he allows people to do their jobs. He's not one of these men who questions every decision people make. I think he feels if he hires responsible employees, he needs to give them the opportunity to be responsible. And do their jobs without interference."

"And do you think he can turn the company around?"

"Yes. And sooner than most people would think," Karla said enthusiastically.

"And I didn't even have to pay her to say all that," Matt joked. "One of the reasons I invited Jeannette to join us for lunch was to benefit from her insight. She'll be working on this project as well. She's lived here all her life, and knows Vancouver and any nuances we might face in dealing with another old city firm. She also has experience in Pacific Rim trading. I value her input."

"Nicely done, young man." Mr. Taylor smiled at his wife. "Women add an aspect we don't always pick up on. I always consult my wife in major decisions. She's a silent partner in the firm. And always has been a major asset.''

Matt met Karla's glance and his eyes twinkled. They already suspected something like this from her talk with Taylor's secretary.

''I'll tell you about our firms' dealings before. You aren't going to like a lot of it,'' Richard said.

''But I'm the one who can change it.''

''There is that.''

Taylor talked at length throughout lunch about the problems he'd experienced with Kinsinger. He and Matt discussed various ways to do business. And he was quick to let Matt know they were not displeased with their new vendor.

Karla watched as Matt was able to glean every bit of information he wanted. The older couple seemed pleased to have their opinion sought so assiduously. And at the end of lunch, when Matt asked if he could meet with them formally in the next week or so to present a new proposal, both acquiesced.

Matt and Karla bid the Taylors farewell in front of the restaurant, watching them climb into a cab.

''How about it, Miss Jones, care to walk back to the office? It's only a few blocks and the weather's warm enough,'' he said as the cab pulled away.

''I'd like that,'' Karla said, falling into step as he turned in the direction of the office building. ''I think it went well, do you?''

''Yes. Better than I might have expected. The order processing department really screwed up a couple of times. And that last batch that was substandard really hurt. I might not have found it so easy to remain as open-minded as they did. But nothing was settled today.''

''I realize that. You opened the door, however.''

''And I want to move quickly on this project. It could really give the firm a boost in the arm—not only monetarily. Morale would pick up with a major new contract.''

''And is morale poor?'' She had seen no signs of complaining or low morale—had in fact thought it on the rise. Of course, except for the new typist she'd hired last week, she didn't spend much time with anyone in the company except as they traipsed in and out of Matt's office. Her workload allowed no time for chitchatting with fellow employees.

''Not that I've noticed. But there is always uncertainty when a new person takes over.''

She nodded, matching her stride to his. She remembered their walk along the seawalk. And his kiss when he took her home after dinner. And last night. Heat washed through her and she wished she could reach out to touch him. Tell him how much she appreciated the chance to work with him. To get to know him. To know him even more than he suspected.

She cringed slightly, feeling guilty. She shouldn't be seeing him socially without being honest with him. Yet, he'd fire her in a minute at this stage. She needed to show him she truly could become invaluable.

But as the day's brightness dimmed a bit, she wondered how she could speed up her timetable to tell him. Maybe it would erase the guilt if she had a definite plan, and a deadline to meet.

''Something wrong?'' he asked. ''You're frowning.''

"No, just, um, trying to remember all I have to do this afternoon."

"When we get back, have Henderson in accounting pull all the records concerning the Percell Group. And call Myers in to review his report. I want a meeting with department heads at three. You, too. Tell them to come with ideas to regain this account. Then do a quick scan and see whom else we've lost in the last year or two. We'll see if we can combine some strategies and regain more than the Percell Group alone."

The office building was in sight. Karla wished for a moment that Matt had talked of something beside work. But why should he? To him, Jeannette Jones was the perfect executive assistant, and dedicated to work. No flights of fancy for her.

He stopped on the sidewalk in front of the huge glass doors leading into the building. "We'll need to work through the weekend on this. I'd like to get back to the Taylors first thing next week. In addition to proposing changes, I want them to know how fast we can respond. Are you available for a marathon session this weekend?"

Here it was—the invitation to the cabin. "Working Saturday?"

"And Sunday. I'll get all the data we need from the department heads. Saturday we can fly up to the cabin where we won't be disturbed. I want to hammer out this proposal completely by Monday. And I want total confidentiality. I want you to handle the typing, not Lisa."

"No problem."

"Good."

Matt held the door for her when they entered the lobby

of the building. "Remind me to tell your niece another reason it makes sense to hire more mature workers."

"What?"

"We had a discussion the other evening about ages of workers," Matt said as he pressed the button to the elevator. "I should have added another advantage of the working relationship between me and a more mature worker—it doesn't bring the sexual tension or innuendoes working with a young secretary would engender."

"Oh?" Karla was puzzled.

"I couldn't take off for a working weekend with some twenty-something young woman. Think of the gossip and rumors."

"Of course." But because everyone thought she was fifty-something, working off-site would raise no comment.

But not everyone believed she was fifty, she remembered when she reached her desk. There in the center was another envelope with her name printed on the front.

She placed her purse over it and smiled at Matt.

"Thanks for including me in the lunch. I felt I learned a lot about strategy."

He nodded, pausing by the door to his office. "I appreciate the response you gave Mrs. Taylor about my management style. I think it went a long way in opening her mind to at least listen."

Karla wished she could bask in the glow of his comment, but as soon as he was seated behind his desk, she put her purse in a drawer and opened the envelope.

Matt Gramling has definite ideas on employee ages. What would he say to yours? For a favor, I won't be the one to tell him.

Good grief, it was blackmail! Karla stared at the note, stunned. What possible favor could someone want that she could grant?

They didn't know her as well as they thought if they believed she could be coerced to do anything wrong at work—even to keep her job.

She needed to find out who was doing this and stop it without causing problems. But where to start?

She didn't want to leave. If she refused to give in to the blackmail, would she have any choice?

Karla bought a few new clothes Thursday evening for her trip to Matt's cabin. Instead of the snug jeans or leggings she preferred, she bought loosely cut, tailored wool slacks. Her normal ribbed tops she eschewed in favor of tailored blouses also cut more fully than she normally wore.

And she bought a huge old-fashioned flannel nightgown that would cover her from neck to toes. Not that she expected a fire in the middle of the night, but she was taking no chances.

She loaded her overnight case with the theatrical makeup she needed. Hoping she didn't give the show away, she was as ready as she could be for the weekend. He'd offered to pick her up, but there was no way she could allow him to pick up Jeannette at Karla's apartment. So she arranged to meet him at the dock.

Friday evening she visited Pat and for a long time forgot the turmoil of her own making as she held and rocked the new baby girl. Holding the precious new child and the glow of happiness between Pat and her husband had Karla yearning for the first time for a family of her own.

Maybe a little boy with dark eyes that watched intensely, or a little girl like Pat's baby, to wrap her father around her little finger.

She refused to give a name to the father of those imaginary children—but Matt's face danced before her eyes.

PLAY

7

Lucky

777

and you can get

FREE BOOKS AND A FREE GIFT!

NO COST! NO OBLIGATION TO BUY!

NO PURCHASE NECESSARY!

**Scratch off the gold area with a coin.
Then check below to
see the gifts you get!**

Lucky 7

YES! I have scratched off the gold area. Please send me
the 2 Free books and gift for which I qualify. I understand I am
under no obligation to purchase any books as explained on the
back and on the opposite page.

386 HDL DNJ9   186 HDL DNJX

FIRST NAME   LAST NAME

ADDRESS

APT.#   CITY

STATE/PROV.   ZIP/POSTAL CODE   (H-R-04/02)

Worth **2 FREE BOOKS** plus a **FREE GIFT!**

Worth **2 FREE BOOKS!**

Worth **1 FREE BOOK!**

Try Again!

Offer limited to one per household and not valid to current
Harlequin Romance® subscribers. All orders subject to approval.

DETACH AND MAIL CARD TODAY!

The Harlequin Reader Service® — Here's how it works:

Accepting your 2 free books and gift places you under no obligation to buy anything. You may keep the books and gift and return the shipping statement marked "cancel." If you do not cancel, about a month later we'll send you 6 additional books and bill you just $3.15 each in the U.S., or $3.59 each in Canada, plus 25¢ shipping & handling per book and applicable taxes if any.* That's the complete price and — compared to cover prices of $3.99 each in the U.S. and $4.50 each in Canada — it's quite a bargain! You may cancel at any time, but if you choose to continue, every month we'll send you 6 more books, which you may either purchase at the discount price or return to us and cancel your subscription.

*Terms and prices subject to change without notice. Sales tax applicable in N.Y. Canadian residents will be charged applicable provincial taxes and GST.

If offer card is missing write to: Harlequin Reader Service, 3010 Walden Ave., P.O. Box 1867, Buffalo NY 14240-1867

BUSINESS REPLY MAIL
FIRST-CLASS MAIL   PERMIT NO. 717-003   BUFFALO, NY

POSTAGE WILL BE PAID BY ADDRESSEE

HARLEQUIN READER SERVICE
3010 WALDEN AVE
PO BOX 1867
BUFFALO NY 14240-9952

NO POSTAGE
NECESSARY
IF MAILED
IN THE
UNITED STATES

CHAPTER SIX

PRECISELY at 7:00 a.m. Saturday morning, she walked down the floatation dock toward the moored seaplane. She had two small cases, one in each hand. The tailored slacks were comfortable, and she hoped baggy enough to disguise her figure. She was getting good at this, she thought wryly. Too bad it wasn't some kind of skill she'd need later in her career.

"Prompt as ever," Matt said as he climbed from the cockpit. He was dressed in dark cords, and the white cable-knit sweater he'd worn last weekend. His hair wasn't as immaculate as in the office, and Karla had that familiar urge to run her fingers through it, just to feel the texture, to connect with him.

That would shock his socks off, she thought, if his staid assistant made a move on him. For a moment she was sorely tempted.

He reached for her cases. "Ever flown in one of these?"

She shook her head, looking at the aircraft with a bit of hesitation as it bobbed on the water.

"A lot more fun than the big commercial planes. Hop aboard." He held his hand for her to steady herself, and motioned to the pontoon.

She could see the skid-resistant patch on the metal and carefully placed her foot on it. The plane tipped slightly when her full weight rested on the pontoon, but Matt quickly assisted her into the tiny cockpit.

She bumped her head on the low ceiling and immediately checked the wig to make sure it hadn't been knocked askew. Hoping everything looked normal, Karla sat in the seat indicated and gazed around with interest.

Matt released the mooring lines and climbed inside, closing the door. The space in the cockpit seemed to shrink. Karla watched as he eased himself into the pilot's seat and began throwing switches.

"When did you learn to fly?" she asked as Matt buckled the seat belt and reached for the earphones.

"When I first got out of the university. It was one of those challenges I couldn't resist. And it's proved beneficial over the years."

"For getting away to the wilderness," she murmured, fastening her own seat belt.

He glanced at her with a puzzled look. "Right. I told you about that?"

She nodded, once again feeling the breath of danger. He had told her, but as Jeannette or Karla? Sheesh, she was getting everything mixed up. How would she keep it all straight?

He started the engines and soon they were skimming over the water of Coal Harbour. Almost before she knew it, they were airborne. Vancouver spread out below them, like a miniature city. Karla was enchanted with the view. That feeling fled instantly when they hit an air pocket and dipped.

"Oh!" She clutched the armrests of her seat. "Are we okay?"

"Sure. No problems," he said with a look. "You've

lived here all your life, tell me what we're seeing as we head north.''

It was easier than she had thought to recognize land-marks from the air, and she was glad to have her mind focused on something besides Matt as they flew along. Not that she could help being aware of him every instant. His fingers were long and lean as he held the controls steady. She remembered how they'd felt caressing her cheek.

His head almost brushed the ceiling and his legs looked cramped. He was taller than she, but when he held her in his arms, the fit was perfect.

Karla could tell by the expression on his face, he loved to fly. And if he had been doing it for almost fifteen years, he must be an accomplished pilot.

Not that she could imagine him being anything but accomplished. If he undertook to do something, she knew he'd make sure he excelled at it.

Making their approach to Henley Island an hour later, Matt pointed out the small settlement where he stocked up on groceries. Making a wide sweep around the end of the island, he lined up the plane and gently set it down on the water, skimming across the surface to a small dock jutting out into the inlet.

"So how did you like it?" he asked as they came to a halt just kissing the end of the dock.

"It was a lot more enjoyable than I expected," she said, her eyes shiny from delight. "I'll look forward to the return trip."

He made short work of tying them to the dock and unloading their bags. Karla reached for hers, but he shook his head.

"I'll take them up."

"Thank you." Turning, she followed the dock to land and then the pathway up the incline toward a log cabin.

When he'd said log cabin, she envisioned something early trappers might have had. Instead, while made of logs, there was nothing cabinish about the place. It stood two stories tall, with soaring windows and a wide front porch extending the width of the house providing plenty of room for sitting out on a warm summer's evening.

"Have you had this long?" she asked, following him up the shallow steps to the front door.

Matt put down the bags and reached into his pocket for the key. "It's not mine. I'm just using it. A friend of mine owns it. But he's in Europe for several months and this way I get a place to use and can keep an eye on it for him."

Inside the house was lovely. The furnishings were old-fashioned, with a warmth and welcome that immediately reached out to Karla. The door opened directly into the living room. She walked in and looked out of the huge window. It was almost as if the outdoors came inside.

Through the trees, she could see the sea. Just the tail of the plane was visible. She smiled and turned. Matt stood watching her.

"It's beautiful," she said.

"I think so. If Steve ever wants to sell, I told him I'll take it. The bedrooms are upstairs. I'll carry your cases up. Do you want to freshen up or anything?"

"I'll just check it out, then be ready to work." She needed to verify everything was in place. She couldn't have her wig tilting over one side.

"Steve has a room off the back I've set up as an office. We'll use that when you're ready," Matt said.

Fifteen minutes later Karla was seated opposite a huge desk from Matt. He plunged right into the task of drawing together a proposal to lure the Percell Group back as a customer.

Time flew by as they worked together—he requesting data, Karla quickly finding it from the various reports they'd brought. When Matt leaned back in his chair and asked Karla's opinion on one aspect, she gave him a thoughtful answer and was delighted when he said he liked it. His incorporating it into the plan made her feel a true team player.

She'd never been involved in strategic planning such as this before and relished every moment. They worked well together—despite her age.

He tossed his pencil down. "I'm getting hungry, how about you?"

"I could eat," Karla said, finishing up her notes. She glanced around at the several stacks of paper with notes on them. "Shall I type these all up this afternoon?" she asked.

"Let's take a break. Working uninterrupted as we've done, we're much farther ahead than we'd be if we were in the office. How energetic do you feel?"

"Very. Sitting all morning, I'd like to walk or something."

"I thought we could walk to town and get lunch at a small café there. The food's good and it would let you see something of Henley Island while you're here. Can't have you coming all this way and only seeing the cabin."

While it sounded like fun, she wasn't sure as Jeannette

how she should react. Shrugging her shoulders, she decided to just be herself. "I'd like that."

And Karla did enjoy herself. Primarily because she was with Matt. The late lunch they ate was delicious. She had chowder with fresh French bread. He had a shrimp sandwich that looked two inches thick.

While they ate, he told her something of the history of the island, how the first settlers, if they could be called that, had been stranded Russian traders. Their boat had been destroyed in a storm and survivors had washed up on the shores of Henley Island.

After lunch, they'd explored the single derelict wooden structure that was the last of the buildings remaining from the first inhabitants.

"I bet they wished they were here now," Karla said, wondering what it would have felt like to be stranded so far from home.

"Why?"

She smiled at him. "Think of the killing they'd make in real estate."

He laughed and Karla's heart hitched. Afraid he'd find it odd to have his secretary staring at him, she forced herself to look away. But the image of his happiness was imprinted on her mind. The day seemed brighter.

It didn't take long to see the entire town. Matt stopped at the small store and bought steaks and potatoes for dinner. Karla teased him about the fare being so typical of what men cooked.

"Never learned the fine nuances of cooking," Matt said. "If you'd rather prepare us a feast?" His look was hopeful, but she laughed and shook her head.

"No, thanks. I love steak."

When they reached the cabin, Matt put away the groceries while Karla headed for the office. She had a lot of things to get typed. Once the first draft was done, they could fine-tune it. By the end of their stay tomorrow, the proposal should be almost complete.

Matt stuck his head into the office. "I'm going down to refuel the plane and run a maintenance check. Do you need anything?"

"No, I have plenty to do," she murmured, not even looking up from the keyboard. She was halfway listening to him and halfway thinking of another way to present this particular concession to make it seem even more important.

Karla lost track of time as she worked. She'd been right to go after this job. After only a couple of weeks, she felt like she was making a contribution—and learning a great deal.

It didn't hurt that she liked her boss. She just wished she didn't have to wear thick makeup and the blasted wig! She had to tell him soon. She hoped he'd admire her boldness for going after what she wanted—and not fire her on the spot.

When the warble from her cell phone first sounded, she wasn't sure what it was. Glancing around, she didn't see Matt anywhere, so reached for her purse.

"Hello?" she said. She should have turned the thing off. What if he came in and she was talking—

"Karla?"

It was Matt!

"Yes."

"How's your weekend going?"

"Fine." Her heart beating, she rose and went to the

door, shutting it firmly. "Where are you?" she asked, knowing he wouldn't tell her precisely enough for her to locate him, but she couldn't take the chance he'd hear her talking.

"I'm at the cabin. Your aunt and I have been working all day on the proposal for a new client. I would have rather stayed in Vancouver to see you."

She walked to the window and gazed out at the lovely scenery. No sign of him on the path to the plane. "That would have been nice," she said.

"Only nice?" Was his voice taking on a more intimate tone?

"Very nice?" she offered.

"Better. What are you doing today?"

She glanced around the office, leaning against the wall. "Catching up on things."

"And what do you plan to do tonight? Do you have a date?"

She knew she didn't imagine the roughened edge to his tone.

"No. I plan to just hang around and maybe work a bit."

"On?"

"This and that. How does my aunt like your place?"

"She likes it. And she continues to be a terrific asset. Didn't waste any time settling in. We took a break at lunch, walked to town and ate there for lunch. Since we've been back, she's been typing up the notes we made this morning."

"Is it a big town?" It was hard to keep straight what she knew and what she wasn't supposed to know.

"No, we walked from one end to another in about five minutes."

"Different from Vancouver, then."

"I'll bring you up some weekend and you can see it for yourself."

Her heart rate sped up. Matt was talking again about bringing her up for a weekend—and not a working weekend like this one was, but definitely a date kind of weekend.

"That would be—" she searched for a word besides the insipid *nice*.

"There's not much nightlife, however. I have to warn you about that."

"I'm sure we could find something to do in the evening. Watch TV maybe?"

"No TV."

"Ah, that is rustic, no matter what you think."

"There is music. We could always dance. I'd like to hold you in my arms."

She swallowed hard. "I like to dance," she said blandly, already imagining them entwined, swaying slowly to sensuous mood music.

"With the right partner."

She smiled. So she might be the right partner?

"We're friends, right?"

"Close friends," he said.

Oops, wasn't that what she'd promised not to do? Not get involved. She couldn't play with fire and not get burned.

"Board games are fun, too," she said. Was she seriously considering going off with a man for the weekend?

No, not any man—Matt.

"Is it wilderness there?" she asked, gazing at the soaring trees that marched to the sea. Not a high-rise building in sight.

"No. Country, but not wilderness. There are some hiking trails. We can walk along the sea. Plenty to do."

"Mmm. Then what are you doing there this weekend working? How do you manage with the lure of the outdoors calling?"

"It isn't easy. The walk to town today with your aunt helped. Want to talk to her? She can let you know her impressions."

Karla almost yelped. She spun around and raced back to her seat, listening intently. Don't let him walk in and find her on the phone!

"No, I don't need to talk to her," she said quickly. "If she's working, she won't like being interrupted."

"Time she took a break."

She could hear him now, in the hallway.

"I've got to go. Um, someone's at the door. 'Bye." She flipped off the phone and plunged it into her pocket. Placing her hands on the keyboard, she was looking at the screen when the door opened to the office. Her heart raced a hundred miles an hour. Matt stood in the doorway, gazing at a phone in his hand, a frown on his face.

Had he heard her voice through the door? She tried to look innocent.

"Hi. How's the plane?"

He dropped his hand to his side and walked to the desk, dropping the phone on top.

"Fueled up and checked out. How're you coming?"

"Almost finished. I've printed out the first section, want to review it now?"

"I'd rather wait until morning. It'll seem fresher for having a break." He seemed distracted as he moved a couple of files to one side.

"Is anything wrong?" The weight of her phone seemed to pull on her slacks. She swallowed, hoping it was fully hidden in her pocket and didn't fall out.

He looked up and caught her eyes. "I guess I didn't think this through. There's not a lot to do around here in the evening."

"I brought a book. I don't expect to be entertained, Mr. Gramling."

He almost smiled, amusement danced in his eyes. "Glad to hear that, Miss Jones. But I don't expect you to shut yourself up in your bedroom when not working."

"I wouldn't mind an early night," Karla said, turning back to the computer. Truth to tell, she couldn't wait to wash her face and take off the wig. Her entire head itched, from her scalp to her cheeks.

As she watched Matt prepare dinner a couple of hours later, Karla wondered how she could bring the topic around to younger employees. His comments during earlier conversations had shown her his bias, and she was at a loss to know how to change his mind. She felt she'd painted herself into a corner and it wasn't going to be easy to get out.

Before she could say anything, he poured her a glass of wine and slid it across the counter to where she sat on one of the bar stools.

"You're easy to be around, Miss Jones."

"Why, thank you." His comment caught her by surprise. "Do you usually surround yourself with people who are not easy to be around?"

He shrugged, taking a glass for himself and sipping the wine. "Not intentionally. But young women seem to like to fill the air with chatter. I find it entertaining for the most part. But there is something to be said for quiet companionship."

She sipped her wine and nodded, hoping she looked wise. She wouldn't mind filling the silence with chatter, but not at the risk of exposing her deception. It was hard to be herself, and not. Yet she wouldn't trade this time with Matt for anything.

"Is that combination of seasonings you anointed the steak with an old family recipe?" she asked.

"Hardly. Any old family recipes I'm likely to have would be beans on toast. My mother died when I was very young and my old man wasn't exactly a gourmet cook."

"You could have learned," she said, wondering what his childhood had been like. How awful to lose a parent when young. Or at any time. She made a note to call her folks when she got home, just to touch base.

"Not my field of interest. And now that I've made a success of things, I can afford to buy my meals."

"Don't you get tired of eating out all the time?"

"Yes. In fact, your niece invited me for dinner this week. A home-cooked meal I didn't have to prepare myself."

"You seem to be interested in my niece," she said slowly.

"Do you disapprove?" He leaned against the counter, keeping an eye on the steaks.

"It has nothing to do with me. I just thought—" Careful, she warned herself. Which one had he told his views of dating?

"Thought?"

"That you weren't interested in a long-term commitment."

"Neither is your niece."

She nodded once. She couldn't tell him at this juncture how being around him had her questioning her long-held beliefs. Maybe there was more to life than getting ahead in business. And while she wasn't truly worried about her biological clock at twenty-eight, if she didn't do something in the next ten years, she would start to worry!

"So tell me a bit about growing up in Ontario. Any siblings?" she asked. Jeannette wouldn't know that, would she?

"No siblings. No family to speak of when I was growing up except my old man. And I left home as soon as I turned eighteen."

"Is your father still living there?"

"No, he died ten years ago." Matt stared into his glass of wine for a long moment. "We were never close. He hit the bottle pretty hard toward the end. I think the booze finally killed him."

"I'm sorry," Karla said, her heart touched by how alone he must feel. No wonder he didn't expect commitment. Not only had Celine let him down, his own parents had done so as well. What would it take for him to change such ingrained beliefs?

Karla excused herself shortly after dinner was finished. She claimed she was tired and wanted an early night, but she couldn't wait to wash her face and take off the hot wig!

Once in the sanctity of her room, she ripped the wig off and threw it on the bed. Heading for the adjoining bath, she soon had the wash cloth in hand and was scrubbing off the theatrical makeup.

"This feels great," she murmured, glad to be back to normal. She donned the long flannel nightgown and slid into bed. She'd read for a while before going to sleep.

But she had just opened the book when her cell phone rang.

Scrambling out of the covers, she ran across the room to her clothes, trying to find the phone before it sounded again. Matt was just downstairs. He'd hear it for sure.

She snatched it up and flipped it on. "Hello?" she said breathlessly.

"Karla, it's Matt."

"Hi."

Tiptoeing to the door, she eased it open a crack and listened. She could hear his voice from the living room, as well as in her ear. Quietly she closed the door.

"No one at your door this time?"

"At this hour?" She crept back to the bed and slid beneath the covers. "Actually, I was getting ready for bed."

"It's only nine-thirty."

"I've had a busy day." She almost laughed, thinking of him downstairs and her up here. She hadn't wanted to leave him after dinner. If she had had his number, would she have called?

"Yeah, me, too."

"Doing?"

"Thinking, drafting up a proposal, entertaining your aunt. She's easy to have around. Not like some people I know."

"I'm easy to be around," she said indignantly.

"Not with the sparks you throw off."

"Sparks?"

"Mmm, remind me to demonstrate when we have dinner next Wednesday."

"If you need reminding, it can't be that obvious."

"Maybe only to me."

She snuggled down in the covers, and reached out to switch off the light. She'd dreamed about hearing his voice in the darkness, now she could.

"So tell me more about this island of yours," she invited.

"I'd rather tell you what we could do when you come to visit. Ever been in a flotation plane before?"

Prior to today? she almost asked. "No."

"We'll fly up along the coast so you can see the mainland from the air. Circle Henley Island to give you an overview of the place. Then land by the cabin. What would you like to do first, go hiking or visit the town?"

"What would you suggest?"

"Ah, a woman who puts herself completely in my hands."

She blinked. Those hands she'd stared at in the plane that morning? What would it be like to be totally in those hands? To have them caress her skin, thread themselves through her short hair and hold her for another searing kiss? She grew warm all over.

"Well, maybe not totally," she said breathlessly. The images dancing before her eyes set her pulse to racing.

"And I thought you were daring."

"I am. In certain areas."

"But not all?"

"Tell me more about this island trip."

"We'll go for a hike first. Walk through the trees until we come to the highest point on Henley. From a meadow on the mainland side you can see almost three hundred degrees. On a sunny day, the sight is breathtaking. I'd kiss you there."

Karla sunk down farther on her pillows. She could almost feel his lips against hers again. Almost taste him, almost reach out to touch him.

"Karla?" His voice was so deep, so sexy. She wished she'd never embarked on this adventure. Would she still have met him at the theater? Would they have found something in common without the problem of work threatening?

"Karla?"

"Hmm?"

"What would you do?"

"Kiss you back, of course. Good night, Matt."

CHAPTER SEVEN

KARLA set her travel alarm early enough to make sure she would have enough time to don her makeup before Matt awoke. She was dressed and ready to descend when she heard him go downstairs. Opening her door, she followed, only to find the place empty. Glancing out the window, she saw him walking toward town.

Wandering into the kitchen, she soon had coffee brewing. Had he gone to get something for breakfast, or should she rummage around and see if she could find something and start preparing the meal?

A hasty glance in the refrigerator assured her there wasn't anything but condiments. He hadn't been kidding when he said he ate out a lot.

When the coffee was ready, she took a cup and went to sit on the porch. It was still cool and she was glad of the thick sweater she'd worn. The wig was like a warm cap, holding in the heat.

The setting was tranquil and serene. She could hear birds chirping in the trees, smell the faint tang of salt in the air. The sun sparkled on the water, and she could just make out the tail section of the little plane. Otherwise there was nothing of mankind to interrupt the flow of nature. No wonder Matt liked getting away. There was a dramatic appeal about the setting.

He had not returned by the time she finished her coffee, so Karla went to the office to double check the proposal they'd drafted. Today they'd fine-tune it and once back at work she'd have time to polish it up for presentation—including the charts and visuals he'd annotated in the margins.

Lost in thought, she didn't hear Matt. But something— a sixth sense almost—alerted her. She looked up to see him leaning against the doorjamb, arms crossed casually over his chest.

"You didn't have to start work so early," he said. "I went for breakfast. I didn't think you'd be up yet."

"I'm a morning person," Karla said, "I always get up early. There's coffee in the kitchen."

"I smelled it as I came in. There are also croissants and rolls in there as well. Care for breakfast?"

"Yes, I'm starved. Your cupboards are practically bare."

"No sense leaving food up here to spoil," Matt said as he led the way to the kitchen.

Their conversation was pleasant and innocuous as they enjoyed the fresh-baked rolls. Nothing like the phone call of last night, Karla thought. She was getting a rare view of how a person reacted with different people. And she liked everything she knew about Matt Gramling.

Matt was critical of the proposal as they reviewed it after eating. He paced the office, challenging everything. Karla tried to remember their strategy and always turned the answer to the best interest of the client, jotting notes in the margin when something didn't come off as strongly as Matt wanted.

At one point he contested a fact and Karla stood, with hands on hips, and gave him the perfect response. He appeared startled for a moment, then swooped in and hugged her, crushing her against his hard frame.

"That's perfect. Absolutely perfect!" Instantly aware, he stepped back, arms dropping to his side. Tilting his head slightly, he looked at her. "Sorry, I got carried away."

Color flooded her cheeks, she knew, but she tried to carry it off with aplomb. "I'm delighted I was able to provide some assistance." Jeez, she sounded like a prig. But, she hoped, a fifty-year-old one.

"We make a great team, Jeannette. You'll be with me when we do the presentation. If you can think as fast on your feet there as here, we won't be stopped."

Pride filled her. She was good at her job, and had a firm grasp of important business goals. Too bad Matt wasn't willing to be as open-minded about younger executive assistants.

It was early afternoon when Matt asked if she could be ready to leave shortly.

"I need to get back to Vancouver," he said, packing his briefcase. Glancing up, he continued, "And you'd have something left of your weekend. I appreciate your help, Jeannette. We finished faster than I thought we would."

"Thank you, Mr. Gramling. I want to be a team player."

He stared at her a moment, then nodded. "I'll be ready to go in about fifteen minutes. Whenever you're ready—"

"I'm already packed. Fifteen minutes will be fine."

She went to get her bag with mixed emotions. She had enjoyed the weekend, especially spending so much time with Matt. And she'd learned more about him, about his family, about what made him the man he was.

But she'd come no closer to finding a way to change his mind about his employee rule. Maybe she could concentrate on that the rest of the day.

She double checked her cell phone to make sure it was off. She didn't want to risk it ringing in the plane.

Feeling like a seasoned traveler, Karla had no qualms about getting into the plane from the dock. The return trip seemed faster than the outward bound one and in virtually no time, they were tying up to the dock in Vancouver.

"I'll have the proposal corrected first thing in the morning," she said, as Matt handed out the suitcases.

"Can you schedule a meeting with department heads as soon as you're finished. I want to review everything and make sure we can live up to our promises. If that goes well, then we'll schedule a meeting with the Taylors. I'll give you a ride home."

Karla had known he'd offer. "Thanks, but I have a couple of errands I'd like to run now that I'm already out. If you could just get me a cab?"

He didn't seem to question how she planned to do errands encumbered with two suitcases, and within five minutes she was safely ensconced in a cab—alone.

Once clear of the dock, she gave the driver her address and leaned back, feeling the relief wash through her. She'd pulled it off! A weekend in close proximity and he'd never suspected!

The relief was twinged with guilt, however. She hated not being as forthright with him as he was with her. Please, let him forgive when she told him. Let him admit his ideas about age were outmoded and she was a perfect executive assistant.

Beyond that, she refused to think. Would he want to count her as a friend once he knew?

Matt entered his apartment and tossed the duffel bag on the floor. He'd unpack later. First he wanted to see if Karla was free.

Punching in the now familiar number, he was disappointed to hear the phone was not in service. Had she turned it off? Or let the battery run down?

He refused to give in to the disappointment. He'd come home as early as he could in hopes of seeing her. Not that he'd given her a hint of that plan last night.

Heading for the kitchen, he pulled a cold bottle of soda from the refrigerator and went to sit on the sofa, legs stretched out in front of him. Sipping the beverage, he thought about last night's conversation.

Her responses had been fresh and forthright. And reminded him of how much he'd enjoyed being with her last Sunday afternoon and Wednesday evening. He wondered if she would really go off for the weekend with him. Could he guarantee it would remain as platonic as the weekend with her aunt?

Restlessly, he shifted on the couch. He did not want to remember his giving Jeannette a hug. Or the reaction his body had felt. For a moment there had been something there. He'd never felt attracted to older women before. It was the excitement of having her nail that particular aspect so strongly. Nothing more.

He took a long pull of the soda, frowning. At least that's all it had to be. He wanted to be able to work with the woman for a long time. He refused to let anything get in the way of that.

But the memory of her feminine body lingered. And the feeling of sexual desire that had filled him disturbed him.

By Wednesday morning Karla felt as if she'd already worked a week. The conferences with the various managers had gone well. Wanting to strike quickly, once Matt learned the Taylors had been available on Wednesday, he'd set the meeting for immediately after lunch.

Today's agenda was all business. The meeting was about to commence. She had her fingers crossed the one o'clock starting time would allow them to wrap things up well before the end of the business day. She had to get home and change before Matt picked her up for dinner at seven.

As she slid into her seat at the polished conference table, she glanced his way. He'd been distant all week, opting for the formality she'd originally tried to instill. She wasn't sure why the change, but it gave her the space she wanted, so she didn't question it closely.

"So nice to see you, my dear," Evelyn Taylor said as Karla sat down.

"Nice to see you, too, Mrs. Taylor. I hope you are ready to be convinced Kinsinger Electronics is the best vendor in town."

"If your enthusiasm is found in the other departments, maybe we will be."

The presentation could not have gone better, Karla thought as the afternoon unfolded. Matt introduced several key managers, brought up each point of contention, and proceeded to demonstrate how the company would deal with each issue. When one or the other of the Taylors had a concern, he often let others handle the response. When Karla answered a particular one and received his smiling nod, she was thrilled.

By four they'd covered everything. Mrs. Taylor looked at her husband. "I think we've seen more than enough to help us make our decision. Shall we be back in touch next week?"

Matt smiled broadly and nodded. "That would be perfect. And in the meantime if any other concerns crop up, please call me or Miss Jones."

Evelyn rose and smiled at Karla. "Thank you, my dear. This presentation has shown me as nothing else could have how much the management of the company has changed with Matt being in charge. I look forward to speaking with you frequently."

Karla almost danced around the room once the Taylors had left and the managers returned to their respective offices.

"Did you hear what she said, Matt?" she asked, her excitement spilling over. "She looks forward to talking with me *frequently*. That has to mean they're going for it, don't you think?"

"Yes, I do. The delay is merely window dressing— and maybe to wring another concession or two from us. Which we factored in. But I think this one is nailed." He stood at the head of the table for a moment. "Would you care to join me in a celebratory drink after work? You did a lion's share of the work on this project."

She was torn. Drinks would be great. Cementing the bond between them. And she had done a lot of the work.

But she needed the time to get home and change.

Noting her hesitation, he picked up his folders. "Never mind, Miss Jones. Another time, perhaps."

"I'd like it another time. But tonight, I have an appointment. I really need to leave at five."

"I understand." He nodded formally and left the conference room.

Picking up the rest of the notepads and folders, Karla knew she'd blown it. He'd never understand. Not unless she confessed all—which she was not about to do yet. Yet how much longer could she continue? Wouldn't it be easier to forgive the sooner the deception ended?

She almost walked into his office to confess all that moment. She'd done well on the project. He had to recognize her skills. And he knew better than anyone she wasn't getting interested in another man. He had no worries about her taking off on some romantic adventure.

But she hesitated. Not yet.

Once the contract was signed. That would be the best time. He'd already given her credit for her part in the project, he'd be in the best mood possible when they signed. She'd wait just a bit longer.

For once fate seemed to be on her side, Karla thought that afternoon when Matt left early. She dashed off for home with extra time to get ready for their dinner date. Her spirits rose now that she'd definitely decided to tell him once the Percell Group deal was signed, sealed and delivered.

She could enjoy their evening without the constant nagging remorse. Not that she could relax her guard, but at least she knew the end was in sight.

He'd be angry, probably. But he had to admit she was an excellent executive assistant, and she was counting on that to enable her to keep her job. That and the aspects she'd contributed to this project.

The flirty dress she donned after her shower was bright red, flaring at the knees, but hugging her where it counted. She carefully applied makeup, fluffing up her short hair and grinning at herself in the mirror. She couldn't wait to see him again.

Watch it, she admonished, trying to rein in the anticipation that soared. She needed to keep control of those emotions. He was a *friend,* someone to share a meal with. At this stage, that was all!

When the doorbell sounded, she almost floated to answer. Matt stood there—a huge bouquet of spring flowers in his hands. She raised his gaze and raised her eyebrows in question.

"For you. I thought the flowers from last week might have wilted by now."

"Thank you." She reached out for the bouquet, her heart somersaulting in her chest. She loved flowers. He'd remembered from dinner last week.

"Come in. I'll put these in water and then be ready. Do you want a drink before we go?"

"We don't have a lot of time. I booked a table at Balcomb's in North Vancouver. I thought we could take the ferry over."

"Sounds great," she called from the kitchen. Finding a suitable vase, she soon had the bouquet arranged to suit her. Carrying it carefully so not to slosh the water, she returned to the living room, placing the vase in a place of honor in the center of her coffee table. Stepping back, she admired the flowers—daisies, tiger lilies, carnations, and several others she didn't recognize. Their bright colors blended beautifully.

"I love flowers," she said softly, her blood humming through her veins when she looked at Matt. How could he look better than he had at the office?

She reached up to kiss his cheek in thanks.

"If I remember, the dock isn't far, and it's still warm outside, want to walk? Or I can get a cab if your shoes aren't suitable," he said, glancing down her legs to the high-heeled shoes she wore.

"Walking's fine. These are comfortable shoes." Just in case there was dancing, though she refused to let the thought linger.

The ferry from downtown Vancouver to North Vancouver was crowded with business people returning home at the end of the day, some still working, others talking on cell phones, and others just sitting. Tourists crowding the rails, excitedly pointing out sites they recognized.

Matt found them a place inside—away from the wind and salt spray, but with a view from the huge windows. He smiled at the elderly woman seated beside them, then turned his attention to Karla.

"Have you been to Balcomb's before?"

"Once or twice. It has the best Italian food in the area, I think."

"It came highly recommended by Richard Taylor."

Karla started to comment, then caught herself. As Karla she wouldn't know Richard Taylor from a hole in the wall. "Is he a friend of yours?"

"New client—I think."

"The big deal you're working on?" she guessed.

"The big deal I think we've cinched." He told her about the presentation and the reaction of the Taylors. Karla listened, touched when he gave her credit for several aspects. He also mentioned the managers who had contributed ideas and data. He might be a turnaround manager, building on the incompetence of others, but he didn't hog the glory. She was fascinated by his persistence in recognizing the contributions in others.

When they reached the dock in North Vancouver, most of the people on board made an immediate surge to exit.

"If we wait a bit, the crush will pass and we can walk off like civilized people," Matt commented, eyeing the crowd.

"I like the way you think. I'm not much for pushing through crowds."

"I remember that from the night at the theater. So we'll wait."

As apparently was the elderly woman beside them. In fact, she was watching the crowd with something like apprehension.

When the majority of passengers had departed, Matt rose and offered his hand to Karla.

"Excuse me, sir," the elderly woman said, rising unsteadily. "This is the only stop here, isn't it? If someone is meeting me, this is where I would get off?"

"Yes, ma'am. This is the terminal in North Vancouver. Is someone meeting you?"

"My grandson," she said proudly. "He and his wife are taking me to dinner for my birthday. I said I'd come here to meet them. They work so hard, they didn't need to come to Vancouver."

"Why not walk out with us, and we'll make sure he finds you," Matt said.

"Thank you."

The three of them slowly made their way off the ferry and to the busy terminal. Passengers were already in line for the return trip.

It was more than fifteen minutes before a harried young man and his wife dashed over to them.

"Grandma! I'm so sorry." He gave her a hug. "Traffic was terrible."

"Hi, Grandma." His companion hugged her and smiled down at the older woman. "We were so worried about you. Did you think we weren't coming?"

"No, this nice young man and his friend kept me company."

Introductions were made, and then Matt and Karla bid the others goodbye and headed for the restaurant.

"I almost thought she'd been stood up," Karla commented once they were on the sidewalk.

"Much longer and I was considering asking her to join us for dinner."

"You had no responsibility for her," Karla murmured, touched he'd already gone out of his way to keep Mildred Williams company as they had. She tried to think of another man she knew who would have done so.

Matt might argue against ties and a family. He might come across as a hard-nosed businessman, dedicated to work and getting ahead. But he had a heart. He'd probably deny it to doomsday, but she knew.

Karla also suspected she could fall for the man in a big way—and she didn't have a clue what to do about it.

The restaurant was not crowded. They were shown to a quiet table which afforded plenty of privacy. Ordering the same entrée, veal scalopini, Matt commented on the fact.

"Great minds run alike, don't you know?" she replied, toying with her water glass. She studied him across the table, her heart catching slightly when his eyes met hers. She felt as if she'd been touched. Her internal temperature soared, staining her cheeks red, she knew, but she couldn't look away.

"So tell me about your day, I've already talked your ears off about mine," he said.

"It was a great day. I got kudos from my boss, and got to leave on time."

He smiled. "And that makes it great? He must be a regular slave driver ordinarily."

"He's a terrific boss," she said seriously. "And I'm learning a lot from working with him."

"Loyalty. A nice trait, Karla."

"So are you renting a flat? Buying a house? What?" she asked, changing the subject before she threw herself into his arms and demand he sweep her away. All from a smile?

"Renting a flat temporarily. I'd like to find a bigger one. With a view of the water, if possible."

The conversation moved easily from Matt's plans for the future, to the musical where they'd met. He casually mentioned seeing another one together soon. Karla liked the fact he easily made plans. He liked being with her, she knew that. As much as she enjoyed being with him?

They were sipping coffee at the end of the meal when he formally invited her to the cabin.

"The one on the island?" she asked, stalling for time. He'd mentioned it before, but now he was asking about this weekend. He wanted her to spend Saturday and Sunday with him on Henley Island. Just the two of them!

"I'll have to check—"

"—my calendar," he finished in unison with her. "You do that and call me tomorrow."

It was hard to concentrate on the conversation after that—when the decision about the weekend loomed. But Karla did her best. The time flew by and it was with reluctance when he mentioned leaving she agreed.

True to his word, they returned to her apartment before ten. He walked her to the door.

"Want to come in for coffee?" she asked, not wishing to end the evening so early.

"I'll take a rain check, if I may." He brushed the backs of his fingers against her cheeks again and gazed into her eyes. "Thank you for spending the evening with me, Karla."

"I had a great time." He was going to kiss her, she knew it. Slowly his head came closer. Seconds before his lips touched hers, she could almost feel him, taste him.

Impatient with his pace, she stood on tiptoes and pressed her mouth against his. The sensations that washed through her filled her with delight. When his arms came around to hold her closer, she relaxed into his embrace, knowing it was almost heaven on earth.

How long could they remain friends? Even good, close friends?

Thursday morning there was another cream-colored envelope in the center of her desk.

"I'm almost expecting them," she murmured as she picked it up and slit it open.

A small favor to keep a big secret. The old boys' network has its referral program, time we did, too!

Karla stuffed it back into the envelope and slipped it into her purse. She thought about asking Lisa if she'd seen anyone that morning, but didn't want the new typist to start speculating why she'd ask. From the last comment, she now knew the sender had to be a woman. But who?

Karla had three choices. First—do nothing. Second, confess to Matt now and hope he was satisfied enough with her work to waive his 25-50 rule—at both ends. Or, third, try to find the person who was sending the messages and make it clear she was not going to cooperate. Her loyalty to the company and to Matt was complete.

And on top of this worry, she still had to decide what to do about the weekend. She spent all day every day with the man, surely it wouldn't hurt to spend a weekend together at the island. The personal time they spent together enabled her to learn precious tidbits of personal information that she alone knew.

And indulge her own desires to be with him. She had never felt so special, so feminine as she did when with Matt. Did he have any idea of the effect he had?

Confessing would probably change everything, she thought morosely. Matt had been very clear he didn't date women who worked for him. Even if he allowed her to remain as his executive assistant once he knew her age, which she fervently hoped he would, he'd stop seeing her socially.

That was enough to give a person second thoughts

about confessing even when she knew it was the right thing to do.

And she had no doubts he'd follow through with his no dating rule. That wasn't even an edict she would argue with him. Office romances could become so tangled.

So this might be the only time she'd have to spend a weekend with him.

She grabbed her cell phone and headed for the stairwell. Checking to make sure no one was using the stairs, she punched in his private number. He answered on the second ring.

"It's Karla," she said, straining to hear if anyone was approaching. It would never do to be caught.

"Did you check your calendar?"

"Yes. I'm free. I would be delighted to go with you to the island this weekend." The die was cast!

"Good." There was a wealth of satisfaction in his tone. "We'll leave early Saturday morning. I'll pick you up at seven."

"Sounds great. See you then." She clicked off the phone, relieved she'd gotten away with the call without anyone using the stairs—not that there was too much risk. Being on the twentieth floor, most people used the elevator.

Focusing on work, Karla decided to ask Pat's advice about her mysterious letters when she went to visit with her and the baby again tomorrow evening. There wasn't anyone else to ask. She just hoped the sender didn't pick up the pace and demand the payoff before Friday.

After dinner, Karla put on the TV and tried to settle in to watch a sitcom. But her mind wandered to the forthcoming weekend. She was about to give up and go do something constructive—like clean her closet—when there was a knock at her door.

Opening it, she was surprised to see Matt.

"I took a chance you'd be home," he said.

"Come on in. I told you I rarely go out on work nights, so it wasn't too much of a chance I'd be here."

"Am I interrupting something?" he asked, quickly scanning the living room.

"No. I was trying to get interested in TV, but it wasn't working. Did you come for that rain check?" She didn't much care why he'd come, she was glad to see him. "I can put water on for coffee."

"Want to go out for a quick dessert? It's warm outside, maybe we could go for a walk along the seawalk, stop for coffee at one of the cafés along the way."

"Sounds great, let me get my jacket." Almost giddy with happiness, Karla was ready to leave in less than two minutes.

"I should have called," Matt said as they headed toward the bay.

"I like spontaneity."

"Good." He took her hand, lacing his fingers through hers. Karla caught her breath, the tingling sweeping through her, making her more aware of everything, from the deepening colors of the sunset, to the feel of the breeze caressing her cheeks.

"I didn't want to wait until the weekend to see you again," he said. "Want to have dinner tomorrow night?"

"I can't. I already have plans."

Matt seemed to withdraw a bit. Stiffly he nodded once. "A date?" As an attempt to sound casual, it failed.

Karla hid a smile, shaking her head. "Not really. I'm going to see my friend and her baby again." Her spirits soared. He cared if she saw someone else. Despite being only friends, he didn't like the idea of her dating! She stepped closer, tightening her hold on his hand and smiling up at him. "I'm glad you came by tonight."

At seven on Saturday morning the doorbell rang. Karla hurried to answer it. She'd packed last night after returning home from visiting Pat and Todd and little Brittany. Rising earlier than usual, she'd dressed quickly and waited impatiently for Matt to arrive. She was excited about the possibilities of the weekend. Two glorious days in his company. It would make up for missing dinner with him last night.

"Good morning," she said with a wide smile, her heart skittering in her chest at the sight of him.

"Good morning to you," Matt said, leaning over to kiss her.

Startled, Karla was swept up into his embrace, opening her mouth to his sweet assault. She'd only caught a glimpse of him—dressed in a black sweater and dark pants. But even a glimpse was enough to convey the sexy, masculine image Matt always transmitted.

He ended the kiss slowly, as if reluctant. Then rested his forehead on hers. "You look lovely."

"How could you tell? I open the door and you give one of your killer kisses."

"Killer kisses?"

"They kill all my good sense."

He smiled slowly, and Karla felt her bones melt. She

was falling in love with the man. What was she going to do?

"I like that."

"Mmm, I bet you do. Are you in a hurry to leave? Want some coffee first?"

"Coffee would be great. I brought breakfast. You didn't eat yet, did you?"

She shook her head. "I don't usually eat much at breakfast."

"You'll love these." He gently urged her into the apartment and closed the door.

"Good grief. Good thing it's early, or there would have been spectators in the hall." She couldn't believe she'd forgotten to even shut the door.

"I knew we were alone," Matt said, heading for her kitchen as if he'd been there a dozen times.

Karla had made a pot of coffee and went to pour them each a cup. The fragrance of fresh-baked bread filled the room.

"Something smells great," she said.

He found a plate and placed the croissants and rolls on it. "If you have jam we'll be set."

They sat at the small table, the morning sun streaming in, his flowers in the center—still fresh and colorful. It was cozy and domestic and almost like a fairy tale, Karla thought as Matt spread jam on his croissant.

One she had best not plan on repeating.

But for today, she'd enjoy the moment. And have the memories forever.

"No morning paper?" she commented, taking pleasure in watching him eat, memorizing his ritual of spreading jam, taking a bite, then a sip of coffee.

"Why would I want to read the paper if I could look at you?"

She laughed. "Do you stay up nights practicing lines to hand out?"

"Only if I think the lady involved would be susceptible."

"And am I?"

"You tell me."

Slowly Karla shook her head. It was a lie. She was as susceptible as the next woman as her fluttering heart attested. But it would never do to let Matt know it. His ego was enormous as it was.

And she must never forget this was but a moment out of time for her. For this moment, she would savor the words and pretend she would change his mind and together they could build a future.

She did have it bad, she thought as she quickly rose to refill the coffee cups.

CHAPTER EIGHT

KARLA felt like an old hand at flying when she stepped into the floatplane an hour later. She balanced easily on the pontoon, and slipped into her seat. The cabin again seemed to shrink when Matt joined her. She could feel her tension rise a notch when his leg brushed against hers as he settled into his seat. Deliberately she'd be willing to bet.

Two could play that game, she thought. Reaching forward to take the earphones he'd shown her how to use last time, she brushed against his shoulder.

"Are these for me?" she asked, leaning forward slightly until her face was only inches from his.

The amusement in his eyes showed he was on to her. But he merely nodded, his gaze dropping to her lips. Karla felt as if he'd touched her. She placed the earphones on her head, her gaze holding his. Slowly Matt leaned closer. Closing the distance, Karla kissed him. Her eyes drifted closed while she enjoyed the texture and temperature and taste of his lips against hers in the gently rocking plane.

"A pilot isn't supposed to drink or take drugs before flying," Matt said, pulling back. "Kissing you is about as intoxicating. If we want to get anywhere today—" he touched her lips with his index finger "—mark my place and we'll take it up again later."

She pursed her lips and kissed his finger. "I've never been intoxicating before."

"Oh, lady, I bet you have. The other guy just didn't tell you. It's a dangerous thing to give a woman a weapon like that."

"But not for you?"

"I love danger."

Karla could understand that. She discovered recently she loved danger as well. Wasn't that what this entire weekend was about?

Feeling almost too keyed up to sit, Karla sat back and tried to enjoy the hour's flight to Henley Island. She had a glorious view of the western border of Canada as they flew north. And a glorious view of Matt when she'd sneak peeks in his direction. She hoped he didn't notice. He seemed caught up in his flying.

When they settled on the inlet near the cabin, she felt a new wave of excitement. This time it was the two of them—with no work to occupy the hours. The enforced intimacy was thrilling. She knew they'd go hiking, maybe have lunch at the café in town. And later—

"Welcome to Henley Island," Matt said, as the plane gently bumped the floating dock. "Hold on a sec, I'll tie up and you can get out."

The air felt balmy against her cheeks as she stepped out of the plane. Matt's hand was there to take hers.

"I hope you have a good time this weekend," he said in a low voice.

Even if they stood all day on the dock, as long as he held her hand, she knew she'd have a great time.

"We'll take the bags to the house, I'll show you

around then we can walk to the village. They have a nice café there where we can get lunch,'' he said.

"So my aunt said.''

"Did she tell you a lot about the island?''

"You might say I saw it all through her eyes,'' Karla said daringly.

"Then you'll have to give me your impressions as we go along, and see how they compare.''

He showed her to the same room she'd had last time and told her to come downstairs when she was ready. Did that mean he had no plans for the dessert he'd alluded to during their dinner on Wednesday evening? Or was he giving her the choice?

Knowing what to expect from the village, Karla had dressed more appropriately to exploring old ruins than she had the last visit. Jeans and sturdy shoes were perfect. The light yellow sweater was enough to keep her warm, without getting hot.

Matt seemed to take as much enjoyment in the exploration as she did. He even stopped in the small general store and found a paperback pamphlet extolling the history of the island. Together they read various sections, and tried to find the original sites discussed.

By the time they stopped for a late lunch, Karla knew a great deal about the stranded Russians and the hardships they'd faced.

"Glad it wasn't me,'' she said as she began to eat the thick roast beef sandwich she'd ordered.

"Glad it wasn't you what?'' Matt asked. He'd ordered the same and was slathering horse radish on his.

"Stranded here.''

"It wouldn't have been so bad. There was game, fishing, plenty of firewood."

"There speaks a true outdoorsman. Drop you anywhere and you'd survive."

He nodded, his expression pensive. "I believe I could. Doesn't mean I ever want to put it to the test."

She nibbled the sandwich as she envisioned him striding out boldly into the wilderness. He fit in that setting as much as in the boardroom. She had never met another man who would.

"So after we eat are you taking me up to that meadow with the terrific view?" she asked.

He raised an eyebrow. "Is that what you remember about the meadow—the view I spoke about?"

She nodded, knowing she fibbed. The primary memory was of his promising to kiss her there.

"I remember something more," he said softly, teasing lights dancing in his eyes.

"Are you suggesting your memory is better than mine?"

"Perhaps a bit more selective. I can refresh yours if you like."

"Maybe." She peeked up at him from beneath her eyelashes and caught the intensity of his gaze. She had no doubts about the meadow and how he'd refresh her memory.

Walking up the hiking trail sometime later, however, Karla wondered if she'd live to reach the meadow. The trail was steep in parts, rocky throughout and narrow. Tall lodgepole pines rose on each side, giving her the feeling she was walking through a roofless tunnel.

But she wouldn't complain for anything. Matt strode

ahead as if on the seawalk in Vancouver. He wasn't even breathing hard! She knew he'd be at home in the wilderness—while she was gasping for breath, and hoping her heart didn't rupture from its rapid pace.

"You all right?" he asked at a bend in the trail. He stood with one foot resting on a rock, the sleeves of his dark sweater pushed up on his arms. His hair was mussed, his eyes sparkling in the sunshine.

"If I live to get to the meadow, I have no doubts I'll find it worthwhile," she said, trying to breathe normally.

He reached out and pulled her up the last few feet. "You could have said something. We can take a rest if you like."

He brushed back a strand of hair, almost caressing her cheek in the process. "We're not in a race. If we want to take it slowly, we can."

"*We* don't need to take it slowly, *I* do," Karla said, surrendering her pride. She took in a deep breath, another. It was good to just stand still for a few moments.

"We're almost there," he offered.

She glared at him. "This had better be spectacular."

He laughed, his head tipped back. She caught her breath, her heart racing for a totally different reason. It wasn't fair that one man had so much charm and appeal. Especially one who reiterated that he was not interested in a relationship.

Lowering his head until he almost touched hers, Matt narrowed his eyes, gazing into hers. He blocked the sun, the trees. Karla could see nothing but Matt, and the power in his gaze.

"I promise I'll do all I can to make sure you find it spectacular."

"The view?"

"Oh? Were you talking about the view?"

Her eyes locked with his, she tried to think of something that would set his blatant sex appeal back a notch or two, but nothing came to mind—except an image of the two of them kissing on the hilltop with the sea around them, and the mainland in the distance.

His finger tipped up her chin, until her mouth was only a scant inch or two from his. "We don't even have to go all the way to the meadow if you don't want."

She could feel the warmth from his finger seep into every cell. Her lips actually tingled in anticipation of his. Did he know the effect he had on her?

"I want to see the view from the meadow," she said firmly. Taking another deep breath, she filled her lungs with the scent of pines, dust, and Matt. It was a heady fragrance that did nothing to ease the tension winding tightly in her body.

"That's all?"

She smiled saucily. "You're the tour guide, surprise me."

The remainder of the hike up seemed easier. In no time Karla walked out into the center of the large meadow. Wild grass grew almost knee-deep. Here and there a brightly hued clump of wildflowers shone in the sun. She could see the sea, the tall trees on the lower slope and in the distance, the Canadian mainland. It was as beautiful a spot as Matt had said.

For a long time, she soaked up the sights and sounds. The hush of the breeze, moving over the grass, causing it to undulate in a mirror image of the waves on the water. Sparkling lights danced on the water. And the quiet was tranquil and serene.

"It's lovely," she said.

Matt stood at her left. He nodded. "I thought you'd like it."

"Is this what you see when you go on your wilderness treks? No signs of mankind anywhere?"

"Usually. Sometimes I discover an old mining camp, or a place where hunters stopped and didn't clean up after themselves. But usually it's just the land the way God made it."

"Wow, no wonder you take off every so often. This is amazing." She wondered if she'd ever get her fill of the view. He'd been right, it was spectacular.

"Want to stay here a little while?" he asked.

She nodded. "Maybe forever."

Matt sat on the grass, stretched out his long legs and leaned back on his hands. "Gets cold at night."

Karla sat down beside him. "You could build a fire."

"Mmm. There are other ways to stay warm."

Tearing her gaze from the view, she looked at him. "And I bet you know them all."

"I know a few. Shall I share?"

Do or die time, Karla thought. She leaned closer. "Yes, share."

Matt pulled her into his arms and lay back in the lush green grass. One hand cradled her head as he brought it in position to kiss her. His mouth was warm and firm and moved against hers with gentle persuasion.

Unnecessary persuasion, Karla thought in the last fleeting seconds of rational thoughts. She reached out to encircle his neck and let the kiss take its course.

Heat to rival the sun swept through her. Passion and desire mingled and grew. She loved this man, loved what pleasure his touch brought. Time seemed to stand still, or spin wildly. She wasn't sure which.

He rolled them over until Karla lay on the sweet-smelling grass. She tightened her hold on him and savored the touch of his hands in her hair, running down the side of her body, pressing her closer to him.

She knew the blazing internal fires he generated would have kept them warm in the most severe blizzard. In the balmy afternoon sunshine, she was burning up. For Matt. With Matt. She'd never felt like this before. It was heaven, it was glorious.

He raised his head and looked at her. She stared into his eyes, seeing the rampant passion he couldn't damp down.

"I want you, Karla, more than I've ever wanted anyone. Are you going to spend the night with me?"

Karla set the table in the cabin, listening to Matt moving in the kitchen. They were having steaks and baked potatoes. His menus weren't too varied, she mused, but delicious all the same.

She studied the table, checking that she had everything. Outwardly she was functioning normally. Inside she was a mass of nervous energy. It was as if her mind was processing at two levels—normal everyday functions, and focused on Matt's question. Was she going to spend the night with him?

She had not given a definitive answer in the meadow. And, instead of being angry, he'd seemed amused. Or was that a cover to hide his own uncertainty?

Hardly. Matt Gramling had not had an uncertain moment since he was five, she'd bet. The man had definite goals, views and opinions and wasn't slow in sharing any of them.

Instead of getting angry, he'd acted as if nothing out of the ordinary had been said. The walk back had been much easier—being downhill the entire way. Conversation had been friendly, and she'd even picked some wildflowers.

Then, they'd checked the plane and she'd helped in the refueling.

When she offered to help with dinner, he'd firmly told her to sit and keep him company but he'd handle everything.

She liked being treated so royally. Kevin had never had her to dinner at his place, they always ate out if they shared a meal. Nor had any of the men she'd dated over the years invited her to their apartments for a meal.

Not that there'd been that many. She had spent a lot of time on her career, and social activities with groups of friends. She knew Pat despaired of her ever falling in love. Wouldn't her friend be shocked to discover Karla had—and with whom?

Last night hadn't been as helpful in solving her dilemma as she had hoped. Taken with the new baby, Todd hovering nearby, Karla had not been able to share everything with Pat as she'd planned. Not that it mattered. In the end, she was the only one to decide what she would do.

Karla touched one of the wildflowers that now graced the center of the table. Glancing around, her gaze was drawn outside. She loved this place. No wonder Matt had come three times already since moving to Vancouver. When his friend returned, would Matt look for a similar retreat?

Seeing him today in the outdoors had given her a new view of the man. She wanted to know everything about him, but realistically knew she'd never see him in his wilderness mode. Still, the things he shared today had given her insight into what he probably was like on his own—man against nature. Strong, calm, resilient and capable. Just about the perfect male.

If only he didn't have that quirky rule about ages!

"Ready to eat?" Matt asked from the doorway to the kitchen—a plate in each hand. In no time they were seated at the table enjoying the meal he'd prepared.

"You are very versatile," she said, slathering butter on her baked potato. "What else, domestically speaking, do you do?" Karla asked.

"This is my limit."

"Surely you don't eat steak and potatoes every night when in the wilderness."

"There, I usually eat what I hunt—small game, or fish. Of course, I always carry a few dehydrated food packs, just in case."

"Have you ever used one?"

He shook his head.

"If you could live any life you chose, would you live in the wilderness all the time?" Karla asked.

"No. I like the challenge of business, the dynamics of turning a faltering concern into a profitable one. And—" he raised an eyebrow "—I think I mentioned, I like women. I don't know any who would relish spending time in the Yukon without any of the amenities we normally take for granted. Would you?''

''Probably not.'' Though if anyone could make it exciting while safe, it would be Matt.

''What would be your ideal life?'' he asked. Holding the bottle of wine, he hesitated over her glass until she nodded. Filling it again, he replenished his own glass and waited for her reply.

''I like the life I have now,'' she said slowly. ''I have a lot of friends to do things with, a job I love, and parents near enough to visit without feeling like they're smothering me.''

''But no steady man.''

She shrugged. ''Is that another misconception you harbor? That women are sitting around waiting for a man to sweep them off their feet?''

''A *rich* man, yes. Want to argue the point?''

''I certainly do! I make a good income, have a nice apartment, and plenty of activities and friends to fill my life. I'm not waiting for some man to come along and change all that!''

''Unless he was rich,'' Matt said smoothly.

''Will you get off that kick? You were burned once. That's too bad. But not all women are like that. Don't you worry about growing old all alone? No family around you? Work can only fill so much of a person's life.''

Matt toyed with his glass a moment, then took a long pull of the wine. ''I don't think about that. If I get to the point where I think a family would be something I wanted, then I'd do what I needed to get one.''

Karla stared at him for a moment. He was serious. Her heart melted for him. What a sad state of affairs. ''Don't do that, Matt. Don't settle for someone who doesn't adore you. You deserve happiness and love.''

He looked uncomfortable. ''I'll keep that in mind.''

''Just because you haven't fallen in love yet doesn't mean it can't happen.''

''Are you in the running?''

She shook her head, trying a smile. ''No thanks. Carefree and liking it that way,'' she said firmly. It was cowardly, but she couldn't tell him how she felt. Even though she wondered what he would say if she told him.

''Ready for dessert?'' he asked.

She felt a kick of adrenaline. Did he mean—

''I can't make a chocolate mousse, but the café in town makes a terrific apple pie. And I picked up some ice cream so I can offer it à la mode.''

''Sounds lovely.''

By the time they finished their dessert, and had some coffee, it was growing dark outside. Matt rifled through a small stack of CDS and placed one in the player.

The soft music filled the house as he held his hand to her. ''Dance with me, Karla.''

She rose with alacrity, delighted to be in his arms. The tempo filled her and she gave in to the swaying her body wanted, moving with Matt, safely held in his embrace.

Song after song played as they danced around the large living room, lost in a world of two.

When the CD ended, he still held her. ''I need your answer now, Karla. Come upstairs with me and stay the night. I want you.''

She looked into his eyes and saw the truth, the sincerity, the passion and desire. No one knew the future. But

Karla knew no matter what it held, memories of a night with the man she loved would always be special.

"Yes," she said softly.

"I'll turn off the lights and lock up," he said, a husky edge to his voice.

"I'll run up and, mmm, change," she said. Her legs would scarcely hold her as she climbed the stairs and headed for her room. Quickly she drew the nightgown she'd brought from the drawer—not the flannel one from the last trip. Trying not to think, to ignore any doubts and second thoughts, she pulled the sweater over her head and in only seconds was ready for the satiny nightgown.

Ivory in color, it was cool as it slid over her skin. The thin straps held it up—but barely. Skimming over her breasts, it fell to just above her knees, a mere slip of a gown, shifting to caress and reveal her body as she walked.

She peered into a mirror, startled to see the glow on her skin, the sparkling lights in her eyes. She already looked well loved.

Spinning around, she took a deep breath and crossed the room to open the door.

Matt leaned against the wall waiting. He didn't know what he was doing, only that he wanted Karla more than he'd ever wanted anyone. She was different from anyone else he'd known. Her laughter seemed to fill him with sunshine. He groaned softly. Did he have a touch of sunstroke? He was sounding as sappy as some damned poet.

She was fun to be with. That was all. And caring. She'd been as concerned for the lady on the ferry as he had.

Loyal. Great, now he made her sound like a favorite dog.

She was— His thoughts fled when she opened her door.

She was beautiful and sexy and slim and satiny soft and smelled like a million flowers. The light in her eyes, the radiance of her smile humbled him. He swallowed hard and pushed away from the wall, drawn to her like a magnet homing north.

His gaze ran down her like a caress. He wanted to touch that silky hair, feel the velvety texture of her skin, slip that barely-there gown from her shoulders and kiss every inch of her.

"You are so beautiful," he said as he reached out his hand to take hers.

He led the way into his room almost wishing the bed was small instead of large. That they'd have to sleep together whether she wanted or not. Would she like to be held all night? The darkness was complete outside, but he could catch the glimmering of stars. He didn't turn on a light, using only the dim illumination from the hallway to show the way.

They should make love outside. He'd love to seek her skin in the starlight. Maybe on another visit—if the summer grew warm enough. He'd wanted to make love to her in the meadow, their meadow, with nothing but the stars to cover them.

Stopping by the bed, he turned her and looked into her eyes, placing his hands on her shoulders. His warm palms heating her cool skin. Taking a deep breath, he held his breath a moment, savoring her special scent before lowering his head to kiss her.

*   *   *

The fragrance of coffee slowly filtered in. Karla rolled over in bed and frowned. Coffee? She opened her eyes. The room wasn't familiar. Then she recognized where she was.

The telephone rang.

She sat up, holding the sheet in place when she realized she no longer wore her nightgown. It had been discarded long ago. Matt was no longer in bed.

Was that her phone? It sounded a second time—and was answered. She looked at the clock on the bedside table. It was only seven, not late. She slid out of bed, looking wildly around for her nightgown. Finding it at the foot of the bed, she put it on. Still feeling exposed, she dashed out to the hall and across to her room.

Quickly snatching up a change of clothes, she headed for the bathroom and a shower.

Dressed a short time later, she sat on the edge of her bed. What was she going to do? Last night had been special. Matt so attentive and loving. And she wasn't really having regrets. Only wishing his feelings for her were as strong as hers for him.

But the morning after was awkward. Did she march down there and greet him like they were longtime lovers? Or wait until she saw how he acted? Should she have stayed in bed waiting for him? Or was he glad she was already up and ready for the day?

They could go hiking again. Maybe have lunch at the café before heading back to Vancouver.

She rubbed her palms over her slacks, knowing she needed to go downstairs, reluctant to move.

Matt rapped on her door. "Karla? Are you dressed? I

have to get back to Vancouver.'' Urgency sounded in his voice.

She opened the door. "What's wrong?"

"There's a major problem with my company in Toronto. I need access to my fax and computer. I may have to fly back there if I can't get things straightened out from this end. Sorry to cut the weekend short, but I need to get to Vancouver as quickly as possible."

"I can be ready in no time," she said, already turning away to pack her bag.

He caught her arm and stopped her, swinging her back gently. "This wasn't how I pictured this morning," he said, lowering his mouth to hers briefly.

"It's okay. I understand business demands," she said. "I'll be ready in five."

"Coffee's ready. Get a cup before we leave." With that, he turned and headed for his room.

At least the awkwardness of the morning was mitigated, she thought, as she folded her jeans and sweater and placed them in the suitcase she'd borrowed from Pat. She had not wanted to take the chance Matt would recognize her own from Jeannette's weekend.

Karla placed her suitcase by the front door and went into the kitchen to get a cup of coffee. She'd have something to eat when she got home. Disappointment about their weekend welled. Yesterday had been so much fun, the two of them shared a lot of interests. Now work intervened.

A thought struck. Would Matt want Jeannette to help out? Good grief, he might have already called to ask her to meet him at the office!

She poured a cup of coffee with shaky hands. There

was no way she would be able to go into the office today. Not after last night. If he had left a message, she would just not respond and make up an excuse tomorrow morning.

"Ready?"

"Yes." She finished the coffee and rinsed the cup. He unplugged the machine, dumped the rest and rinsed it with water, leaving it to drain on the side of the sink. With a quick look around in farewell, they headed for the plane.

In no time they were airborne and heading for Vancouver.

CHAPTER NINE

KARLA stared out the window, at the sea, at the scattering of smaller islands that dotted the expanse of ocean. A jumble of emotions swirled around inside. She closed her eyes in memory of last night. Matt had been so incredibly tender—and so amazingly sexy she couldn't believe it. Their lovemaking had been fantastic—and had topped off her love with feelings so strong she wondered if she would ever get over the man.

She knew last night's memory would always be special. The wealth of love she'd poured out, the kisses that had been so potent, his caressing hands, her own. His scent, and taste and touch. All were burned into her mind for all time.

"You're quiet today. Regrets?" he asked.

Opening her eyes she looked squarely at him. "None. You?"

"Only that our weekend got cut short. We'll have to go away again."

She nodded, smiling warmly. "I'd like to see the meadow again. But before next time I'm practicing so I can climb up there without going into cardiac arrest."

He nodded, reaching out to take her hand, resting their linked fingers on his hard thigh. "I appreciate your not throwing a fit at the way the weekend turned out."

"I understand business demands, Matt." What had his

other women been like if they threw a fit when a crisis arose?

"I hope the crisis at your company is easily resolved."

"We'll see. I need to get all the facts before proceeding."

She could almost see him click into business mode. She gazed out the window, feeling dismissed, yet linked by their hands. His palm was warm, firm against hers. His thumb absently caressed the back of her hand. A small thrill raced through her. His touch was still potent, and sexy. She wished the business problems had not arisen. She felt cheated of their day together.

When they docked in Vancouver, she took her small bag and walked along the pier with him. "I'll get a cab home. You can head right for work."

"I'll take you."

"No need. I know you need to get in and start the ball rolling on that problem." She stopped and looked up at him. "I had a great time."

He smiled. "You sound like a proper little girl being polite."

"I was properly brought up and I am being polite. And honest. I had a great time."

He brushed his fingers against her cheek and caught the nape of her neck, caressing gently, his palm warm and firm. "I don't want this to be our only weekend."

She smiled and nodded, afraid to speak. How many could they have? She felt another twinge of guilt. Before she went again, she'd make sure he knew everything. It wasn't fair to Matt or to her to continue they way they'd been. And it was up to her to make everything right.

He kissed her gently. "I'll call you."

"Okay."

He signaled for a cab and put her inside, handing the driver some bills.

Karla glanced out the back window as they pulled away, Matt was already striding down the street in the direction of the office building. Business came first.

When Karla reached her office Monday morning, Matt was already on the phone. She waved through the open door and went to her desk. Lisa arrived a short time later and Karla heard her starting work.

Reviewing the things she had left from last week, Karla kept an eye on the phone. As soon as Matt got off, she'd go in for their routine morning planning session. She was impatient to learn what had happened in Toronto, and if she could help.

But the minutes ticked by and he remained on the phone. Was the call connected with the problem in Toronto? It had to be. At least he hadn't had to go east to deal with it.

When Karla's phone rang midmorning, she answered it unsuspecting.

"Are you going to grant a small favor?" an unfamiliar voice asked.

"Are you the one sending me anonymous notes?"

"I know who you are and the stunt you're pulling. But if you help me, I don't have to blow the whistle."

"What is it you want?"

"The job available in Human Resources."

"Pat's job?"

"Yes. They're considering two other people. But a few good words put in by you, and I bet Mr. Matthew

Gramling will throw his weight my way. At least you better make sure he does.''

''Who are you?''

The hesitation on the other end was noticeable. Finally the woman said, ''Alice Sawyer. I've been here for six years. It's time I was promoted to department head. You fix it and I'll keep quiet.'' She hung up.

Karla replaced her phone and glanced around guiltily. Matt was still on the phone and from the sound of typing in the outer office, Lisa was fully occupied.

Quickly Karla dialed Pat's home phone.

''Hello?''

''Pat, this is Karla.''

''What are you doing calling me at this time of day? Boss out of the office? You're lucky I was home. Brittany and I are venturing out today for the first time. For a doctor's checkup. I guess it's okay, or they wouldn't have scheduled it, but she's so tiny and—''

''Pat! I need some information and I can't talk for long.''

''Oh, okay. Shoot.''

''Do you know an Alice Sawyer?''

''Of course, she worked for me when I was at Kinsinger. Why?''

''She wants your job.''

Pat laughed. ''Yeah, she's wanted to be promoted from almost the first day she started. The problem is she doesn't retain anything. She's all right for filing and some basic work, but try to explain benefit procedures, or retirement options or general labor law to her and it's like talking to a wall.''

"She thinks she can be head of Human Resources here."

"She's wacko. How are you involved?"

"She knows I'm not a fifty-something woman working for the big boss and is threatening to blow the whistle unless I fix it for her to get the job. She seems to think Matt would be swayed by my opinion."

"Whoa. Karla, that's bad. If she's trying something like blackmail, she can't be trusted in the department."

"You don't think I would recommend her, do you?" Karla asked.

"No. Wait a minute, I'm thinking. I bet she got your age from the personnel records. She does our filing. Guess she's bored enough to read the applications. But she's supposed to hold things like that confidential."

"Well she's threatening to tell, but maybe she won't— it could be all bluff. Anyway, I thought I'd check with you about her. I'll have to find a way to tell Matt the truth before she makes good her threat."

"Karla, I can't believe you got away with it for this long. He's going to go ballistic when you tell him."

"You might be right. I'm just hoping he'll listen with an open mind. I have done a great job—he can't deny that. Damn, this timing stinks. I wanted the Percell Group deal signed first."

"Call me when the dust settles and let me know how it went."

"Okay. Kiss the baby for me." Karla hung up.

Now what? Try to find a moment to speak to Matt to spike Alice's guns? Or should she try to talk to the woman once more?

Matt stood in the doorway to his office. "Jeannette,

call the Taylors and see if they've decided about the proposal and if so schedule a conference for tomorrow morning if they can make it. Then get me a flight tomorrow afternoon to Toronto—return on Sunday. Cancel anything I have scheduled for the rest of the week.''

''So you have to go?'' she said.

He nodded. ''You heard?''

Karla looked away, forgetting his secretary hadn't heard, his date had.

''From Karla,'' she said.

''I'll need a car and a place to stay close to the office there.'' He turned back and before she could ask him about getting together to review things, he was back on the phone.

She called Mr. Taylor, but he was unavailable. Leaving a message, she jotted herself a note to follow up later in the day if he didn't call back.

Karla watched the rest of the morning for an opportunity to speak to Matt, but he remained incredibly busy. Faxes poured off the machine in Lisa's area and she dutifully brought them in instantly. Karla knew Matt was directly linked to the Toronto office on his computer and with the phone constantly at his ear, he was unavailable for anything else.

She took a late lunch and returned to the office to find Lisa back at her desk, but Matt gone.

''Mr. Gramling went out for something to eat,'' Lisa said. ''I have most of those papers done he wanted. But he gave me two tapes to transcribe this afternoon, so I can't get to that other project.''

''He knows his priorities. Don't worry about the project, it'll keep.''

She stepped into her office and stopped. A young woman of about thirty was sitting in the guest chair. She glared at Karla.

"Alice, I presume," Karla said, wondering if she should shut the door between her office and Lisa's work area. She never had—would it cause comment? How much could Lisa hear if she didn't close the door? The sound of the keyboard rattled behind her. Hopefully Lisa was fully occupied with her tapes.

"I can see how he was fooled," Alice said, standing. She wasn't very tall, and her attire was casual for business. "Are you going to tell him I'm the best for the job?"

"I can't do that," Karla said. "I spoke with Pat Carns after you and I talked this morning. She says you aren't qualified."

"I've been working at that job for six years! I know everything that goes on around here. I had you figured out, didn't I?"

"There's more to the position than that. What about payroll regulations, labor law, benefits, things like that."

"There are a lot of people in the department, each one specializes in one aspect. I would be the manager. I don't need to know it all, that's what they're for!" Alice said hotly. "I want that job and you can help me get it."

"No, I can't. Even if I thought it would do any good to recommend you, I couldn't do it. It's not right."

"What you're doing isn't right. It's lying and cheating and wrong. But you went ahead anyway. Why are you standing in my way? *I want that job!*" Alice was almost yelling.

Add emotionally instable to the list, Karla thought

wryly. And her own experience wasn't so extensive that she knew how to defuse the situation.

"Shh. Yelling about it won't change anything."

"I'll yell if I want! You had better help me or I'll make sure Gramling knows everything there is to know."

"And that would be?" Matt asked from the doorway. Lisa stood behind him, peering in, her eyes wide with shock.

Karla spun around in horror. How much had he heard?

Alice glared at him.

"Perhaps we should take this discussion into my office. I could hear you from the elevator."

"I can explain," Karla began.

"I can do my own explanations!" Alice said.

"Inside my office, both of you." Matt's tone would not be denied.

He waited for the two women to precede him, followed, and closed the door. Moving to one side he folded his arms across his chest and looked from one to the other.

"I don't know you," he said to Alice.

"Alice Sawyer, from Human Resources," she said grudgingly, glaring at Karla.

"What's the problem?"

"There wouldn't be any problem if Miss Jones would recommend me for the manager's position."

"The opening in HR?" he asked.

Alice nodded.

Karla could only stand, dreading the explosion that would erupt if Alice didn't keep quiet.

"Aren't there channels to go through to apply for a job? Why come to my executive assistant?"

"She owes me," Alice mumbled.

"I do not!" Karla said.

"Why is that?"

Alice looked at Karla. "Are you going to recommend me?"

For one second Karla wished she could. Wished she could do something that would stop the tidal wave that threatened.

Slowly she shook her head. "I can't do that."

With a sly look Alice shifted her gaze from Karla to Matt.

"That woman is an imposter. I don't know how she's fooled you all this time, but she isn't any more fifty years old than I am. A wig, makeup and dowdy clothes don't mean she's who you think she is." Her triumphant expression made Karla want to slap her. She'd done it. She'd told Matt!

Matt looked at Karla.

She met his gaze, startled at the anger that flared. He stepped forward and looked at her hair, reaching out to pull the wig from her head.

"I can explain," she said quickly.

He snatched the glasses from her nose and tossed both on his desk.

"Karla Jones. Not Jeannette." The coldness in his expression was frightening.

"If you'd listen to me for a minute, I can explain everything."

"No explanation necessary. Not from you. Nor you, Miss Sawyer."

He opened the door. "Lisa!"

She appeared instantly. "Yes, sir."

"Call security to escort these women from the premises."

"Matt, no!" Karla said, horrified. "Let me explain."

"As of this moment, you no longer work for Kinsinger Electronics. Either of you. You're both fired."

Matt closed the door behind the departing contingency several moments later feeling furious. He strode to the desk and snatched up the offending wig, balling it tightly he flung it across the room.

He was seething with anger.

He stalked to the window, hoping the sight of the sea would sooth somewhat. But he could still feel the shock of discovery.

Jeannette was Karla.

Or vice versa.

And some woman in the Human Resources department tried to blackmail her for advancement. God, what a mess!

Unbelievable.

How could she have done it!

And how could he have not seen it?

Which made him more angry, he wondered dispassionately, the fact she'd pulled it off, or that she'd tried to begin with? Or the fact he'd believed in Jeannette?

There was a light tap on his door.

"Yes?" He turned as Lisa poked her head inside.

"There's a call for Miss Jones. I didn't know whether to take a message or not."

"Who is it?"

"Oh! I don't know. I can ask."

"Never mind, I'll take it." He reached for the phone

as she closed the door. He'd never noticed how timid Lisa was before. Of course, she worked for Jeannette—Karla, would she be able to run things as smoothly?

"Gramling."

"Hello, Matt, Evelyn Taylor here. I was trying to reach Miss Jones. She called earlier about setting up another meeting."

"Miss Jones no longer works for the firm. I need to go out of town on business this week, but wanted to touch base with you and Richard before I left—to see if there were any other aspects of our proposal you had questions on. I'm hoping you are ready to sign."

"What happened to Miss Jones?" she asked.

He scowled and turned back toward the window, hoping the anger didn't show in his tone. "She was dismissed today."

There was a moment of silence on the other end. "Fired?"

He couldn't believe it himself. He rubbed his forehead. "Yes."

"Why?"

What possible business was it of a possible customer to know about the personnel problems at his firm? Not something conducive to instilling confidence. Still, he could hardly tell her it was none of her concern. That'd go over well.

"Turns out Miss Jones wasn't quite what she purported to be. She is not in her fifties, but somewhere around twenty-five."

"So?"

"So I hired a mature woman, and got an imposter."

"What were her reasons for the impersonation?" Evelyn asked, curiosity obvious.

"I don't know."

"What was her explanation?"

"There was none. I didn't need to hear any cock-and-bull story to mitigate the damage. When I discovered the deception, she was history."

"You fired her on the spot and gave her no chance to explain?" Evelyn's voice cooled noticeably.

"Exactly." Why did hearing it from Evelyn make it sound like a poor decision? He was decisive. When he made a decision, he didn't second guess it after the fact.

"I see."

"As I said, I have to leave town tomorrow, but would like to schedule a meeting with you and Richard before I go. Or if that won't work, how would next Monday suit?"

She was quiet for another moment, then spoke again, "I'll talk to Richard and we'll be in touch. Goodbye." She hung up.

He opened his door and called for Lisa.

She rushed in, looking flustered. Similar to the way his secretary in Toronto often looked.

Neither had the calm demeanor Jeannette—Karla—had always shown.

"Get the head of the HR department up here to discuss this situation. Check on my reservations, I'm leaving tomorrow afternoon for Toronto and should have an open ticket so I can return when I'm ready. Make sure I have an updated version of the Taylor project folder to take with me."

"Okay." She looked positively petrified. "Where is the Taylor project file?"

"Look on Miss Jones's desk."

He watched her for a moment, scrambling the neat piles Karla had stacked on the surface. Impatiently, he crossed to the desk and found the folder in only seconds.

"Sorry. I'll call HR." She fled for her desk.

Matt knew it was going to prove a long afternoon. For a second he almost questioned his rash act. But seeing the glasses lying on his desk strengthened his resolve. She'd played him for a fool—at work and in their personal lives. He wouldn't forget.

The next Monday afternoon, Karla entered her apartment, more tired than she had been a couple of weeks ago after a long day at Kinsinger. Interviewing was hard work. She kicked off her shoes and padded in her stocking feet to the kitchen to get a glass of water. She refused to let herself become discouraged. It had only been a few days.

Of course she'd spent that first day alternating between rage and tears. Angry that Matt had not let her explain, and upset and sorrowful he'd let her go like that. Not caring enough to even ask why. She sure had him figured wrong.

She glanced at her answering machine as she walked back into the living room. The message indicator light was flashing.

A callback maybe from her Friday interview? That one had gone well. She pressed the button and caught her breath when a familiar voice sounded.

"Karla, Matt Gramling. Call me."

There was a second message. "Karla, Gramling here. Call me. I'm at the office."

And a third. "Karla, where the hell are you? Call me."

All three calls since nine that morning.

"Well that's surprising," she murmured as she crossed to the sofa and sat down, sipping more of her water. He kicked her out last week without a chance to explain and now called her and almost ordered her to contact him. Didn't he realize he was no longer her boss?

"So what's up, Mr. Gramling, that you're calling me? Had second thoughts and want to hear my side? Missed your effective executive assistant?"

Karla stared at the answering machine as if it could give her answers to her questions.

She could call and find out. But was she ready? Tears filled her eyes and she blinked them away. He'd been so harsh and unapproachable. To refuse to give her a chance to explain was inexcusable. She'd expected more of him. He'd been fair to others, why not to her?

"You can just wait a bit longer, Mr. Gramling," she told the machine. "Until I'm good and ready to talk to you. Or hell freezes over, whichever comes first!"

Rising, she went into the bedroom to change into casual clothes.

The phone rang. Karla's heart leaped, but she remained in the bedroom, straining to hear the machine.

"Karla, Gramling here. Call when you get in."

There was definitely impatience in that tone, she thought wryly. The head of Kinsinger Electronics was used to people jumping to do his bidding. She almost laughed. He didn't like being kept waiting.

"And I don't like being blown off like you did. You

should have given me a chance to explain,'' she said, walking back into the living room and erasing the messages on her machine.

On to the kitchen, she tried to decide what to prepare for dinner. Tomorrow morning she had another interview scheduled and wanted to make an early night of it. Not that she'd sleep. But she could make the effort.

Twice more during the evening Matt called. The final time his tone changed.

''Karla, I know you have to be home by now. Pick up…Please.''

She knew the word please had been an afterthought. Hesitating, she heard him continue.

''I need your help on the Percell Group project.''

She lifted the receiver.

''So because you need some help on a project, I should forget the way you treated me last week and leap at the chance to come to your assistance?'' she said.

She heard his indrawn breath as if he were trying to find some patience.

''Evelyn Taylor has this bee in her bonnet that if I'm so ruthless I wouldn't even listen to an explanation, I'm not the kind of businessman they want to deal with. There are other deals out there, but this one would be immediate, and show the employees we are turning things around and moving forward. We worked hard on it. I want this deal consummated.''

''So?''

''So I need your help. The Taylors have agreed to another meeting to hammer through things—but only if you are also there. You owe me.''

''You're kidding.''

"No, dammit, I'm not."

Karla could almost feel the seething rage in his answer. She did not owe him!

"So how does my being there help?"

"It'll show them I'm flexible. The company will respond to their concerns in a rapid fashion. I don't know, she just won't come unless you're there."

For a moment Karla wondered why Evelyn even cared. "I'll consider it on one condition."

"And that is?"

"You give me a chance to explain and listen to me—really listen to me."

"After the deal is signed."

Once that had been her timetable as well.

"No, after the meeting—win, lose or draw with the Taylors—you listen to me." She wasn't going to be blown off a second time.

"Deal. Can you be here in the morning at ten?"

"Is that when the meeting is scheduled?"

"Yes."

How like him to schedule it and then see if she could make it. She'd have to postpone her interview, but for the chance to tell Matt why she'd pretended it would be worth it. "Okay, I'll be there at ten. But I'm warning you, I'm coming as Karla. You still have my wig."

"I trashed it."

Great, now she owed Polly a new wig. Maybe she'd request Matt pay for it.

Good grief, she must be growing giddy with the thought of seeing him again. There was no way in the world he'd pay for the wig. She'd be lucky if he'd give her five minutes to listen to her explanation.

Would it change anything? Would he offer her the job again? Invite her to dinner one night?

"I'll be there by ten." She hung up before he could say anything further.

So Matt needed her to clench the Percell Group deal. What was Mrs. Taylor up to?

Right before ten the next morning, Karla pressed the button for the express elevator. She wished she'd listened to Pat at that fateful lunch several weeks ago and not considered it fate when she'd learned of the open executive assistant's position. Then if she and Matt had met at the theater, she could have considered that fate.

And been no farther ahead, she thought, her heart speeding up in anticipation of seeing him.

Hope was hard to kill.

When the elevator reached the executive floor, Lisa was waiting. She greeted Karla with relief.

"Oh, Miss Jones, I'm so glad you could come. He's been absolutely horrible. So demanding, and I can't find anything! I'm glad to do all the typing, but you always handled everything else."

She led the way to Karla's office, talking as fast as she could, as if to dump all her aggravation on Karla in the short distance and span of time she had.

"Do the best you can. Surely he's interviewing for my replacement," she said with a pang when she saw her desk. It was *her* job. She'd given it her all, and loved it.

And, if nothing else, she had planned to see Matt through the years at work, knowing a long personal relationship was impossible. It would have been enough. Maybe.

"Not yet. He was in Toronto until yesterday. But I can tell you, another day like yesterday and I'm history!"

Matt opened the door to his office. Lisa gave a small yelp and scurried away. He glanced at her, then at Karla, his gaze tracking from her short sassy hair, down the fitted navy dress, suitable for office wear, yet nothing like the staid clothes Miss Jones wore.

"She might be a great typist, but she can't do anything else."

"That's all she was hired for." Karla slowly took a deep breath, trying to calm her roiling nerves. He looked tired, as if he hadn't slept in days. Her heart lurched.

"How are things in Toronto?" she asked.

His expression tightened. "None of your business."

She should have expected it. Placing her purse on the desk, she faced him. "So what do you want me to do for this meeting?"

He rubbed the back of his neck. "I don't know. Look like you work here again. Tell Mrs. Taylor that we've ironed things out and I'm flexible and willing to listen."

"Lie to her, you mean?"

He glared at her, "Why not, you're good at that."

She raised her chin. "I never lied to you. Everything I said was truth. Check my application form."

"You said Miss Jones was your aunt."

Shaking her head, she responded, "No, you said that, I didn't correct you."

"A technicality. And not the issue I need to deal with first. The Percell Group account takes priority."

"But you and I will talk afterward," she said firmly.

CHAPTER TEN

"MISS JONES?" Lisa peered around the door. "The people from the Percell Group are here. I put them in the conference room."

"Thank you, Lisa. We'll be right there," Karla said calmly. She glanced at the desk then back to Matt. "Do you have the folders and spreadsheets you need?"

"In my office. Took Lisa half a day to find it all."

Karla kept quiet, knowing he could have called her or had Lisa call her, to find whatever they needed. Sometimes stubborn pride deserved hardship.

"So I pretend I'm your executive assistant for the duration of the meeting. That all?"

"That should be enough."

"Fine." She gathered a notepad and a couple of pens and headed for the conference room, conscious of Matt's gaze fixed on her until she left her office.

Evelyn and Richard Taylor greeted her warmly when she joined them in the conference room.

"How nice to see you again. Oh, my, what a difference," Evelyn said, as she took in Karla's changed appearance.

Karla flushed at the scrutiny, embarrassed to be caught out by this nice couple. "It is easier to keep up," she said weakly.

"You haven't met our son, Ashbury. He's going to be taking the reins one of these days. I thought he should be in on our meeting,'' Richard said, stepping aside so a tall young man could offer Karla his hand.

''Delighted to meet you, Miss Jones. I understand there has been some problems with your employment.''

''I can't wait to hear why you thought dressing up as if you were an old lady was necessary to get a good job,'' Evelyn said. ''I spend a fortune each year trying to look younger than I am.''

''It was because of the twenty-five/fifty rule,'' she said just as the door opened again, admitting Matt.

''I don't believe I know that rule,'' Evelyn said.

Karla moved to take a seat down from the head of the table. ''I'll explain later,'' she murmured, hoping Matt hadn't heard.

Once greetings had been exchanged, and Matt had met Ashbury Taylor, everyone sat and the meeting began in earnest.

Richard Taylor questioned certain aspects of the proposal as presented and Matt easily cleared up the concern. He and Ashbury Taylor discussed delivery dates and contingency plans if problems arose. Evelyn said nothing, merely watched from the sidelines.

The meeting wound up before noon, with a promise of a major contract to be signed as soon as the attorneys drafted it—incorporating all the points agreed upon.

Karla wondered what her purpose had been. She, like Evelyn, had said very little. But she'd noticed Matt's gaze more than once. And Ashbury Taylor's.

As the Taylors were preparing to leave, Ashbury came over to Karla.

''Are you free for lunch? I'd like to discuss a possible

position with our firm. Unless I'd be stepping on toes somewhere?''

"There are no toes to step on," she said. "But, um, you might hesitate if you knew the full story about my employment here.''

"I can't wait to hear it, but anyone who goes through all my mother talked about to land a job shows determination and gumption. Something we value at Percell Group.''

Matt heard. His glower could almost be felt.

Karla ignored him, smiling brightly at Ashbury. "I'd be delighted to have lunch with you.''

"May I see you a moment," Matt said, taking her upper arm in a grip that wouldn't easily be broken. He practically marched her from the room into the hallway.

"What are you doing?" Karla asked in startled surprise.

"I thought you and I were going to have an explanation session. Now you're flirting with a customer?''

"I'm not flirting," she hissed, pulling herself free. She glared up at him. "It won't take five minutes to give you an explanation. And if there is a possible job opportunity, I need to investigate it. He's not my customer—unless you're offering me my job back here?''

Matt shook his head once. "Not a chance, sweetheart.''

"I didn't think so. That makes me free to seek other employment. And you can't stop me.''

"Mr. Gramling," Lisa said behind Karla. "Your assistant in Toronto is calling. She says it's important. I told her you were in a meeting, I didn't know you were already finished. But she said I should get you. Can you take the call?''

''Of course I can take it, tell Sarah I'll be there in a second.''

''Don't let me keep you,'' Karla said.

''And your burning desire to give me that explanation?'' he asked silkily, his eyes narrowed in frustration.

''It's waited a week, what's a little more time.'' Karla knew no matter what, he wouldn't change. Hadn't his last comment proved it? Did it matter if she told him why she'd tried to look older. It wouldn't alter anything.

''Wait here. I'll see what Sarah wants and then I'll take you to lunch.''

She blinked in surprise. ''Why would you do that?''

''Damned if I know.'' He stepped around her headed to his office.

Karla watched him walk away, puzzled by the invitation. Longing to accept, she thought she'd do better to explore new opportunities. ''I can't,'' she said softly to the empty hall. ''Much as I want to, I can't.''

She turned and reentered the conference room. The Taylors were ready to leave, and when Evelyn pressed her into joining them for lunch, Karla accepted. They were nice people and they might offer her a new position somewhere.

Despite her best intentions, Karla regretted not waiting for Matt. Lunch was delightful. And Ash, as he'd asked her to call him, had come through with a job opportunity. She was going to the Percell Group offices in the morning for a formal interview, and to see their offices.

Evelyn had been totally entertained with the reason for

her acting older, and asked Karla if she minded if she told some of her friends.

"I'd rather you didn't," Karla said slowly. "I wouldn't do anything in the world to jeopardize Matt's image in the business community."

"Loyalty is a valuable commodity. I wonder if Matt realizes he still has yours?" Richard asked.

He had more than her loyalty, she thought, he had her love. But he wanted neither.

After lunch she'd taken a brisk walk along the seawalk, enjoying the fresh air and the breeze that danced across the harbor. She tried to ignore the memories of walking with Matt. Just over a week ago they'd had dessert at that little café.

She sighed and tried to forget. It wasn't easy. But Vancouver sparkled in the sunshine, and her spirits gradually rose.

By the time she returned to the apartment, she felt better than anytime in the past week. She changed into old jeans and a T-shirt. Going barefoot into the kitchen, she rummaged around for something to eat. Living alone, she didn't often cook for herself, but ate her main meal at lunch to get at least one good meal a day.

She'd been disappointed when she first entered the apartment to notice the answering machine had no messages. She'd hoped Matt had called. He'd have been angry at her, no doubt for standing him up for lunch. Which would have been the perfect reason for him to call—if only to yell at her.

Glancing at the clock, she saw it was almost five. Too late to call him to arrange a time to give her explanation.

She'd phone first thing tomorrow, before heading out for her interview at the Percell Group.

The knock on the door startled her. Wondering who it was, she crossed to answer. Opening the door, she was totally dumbfounded to see Matt Gramling.

"We need to talk," he said, pushing his way into the apartment. "And you're not walking out this time."

Karla closed the door and leaned against it. Thinking of all the other outfits she had she could have worn, why was she in faded jeans and a baggy old T-shirt? Her lipstick had worn off and she knew her hair was tousled from the wind.

"Thanks for the advance warning," she mumbled, pushing off from the door. Matt had slung off his jacket and tossed it across the back of the sofa, sitting on one end as if he owned the place. Karla crossed the room and sat gingerly on the edge of a chair.

"What warning?"

"If I had known you were coming, I'd have— Never mind." She wasn't about to tell him she cared how she looked. No telling what he'd think with such a confession.

But it wasn't fair. He looked terrific. A bit leaner than she remembered, and tired. But the same intensity shone in his eyes. The same broad shoulders she'd once thought could hold the world filled his shirt. The same fluttering in her heart told her immunity against him was a long way off.

"I told you I'd take you to lunch," he said.

She shrugged. "I decided to go with the first invitation."

"Did they offer you a job?"

"Is that any of your business?" she asked, still hurt from his brusque response to her question about the Toronto problem.

"I'm making it my business. In fact—" He took a breath, rose and paced to the window. Turning, he looked at her. "In fact, if things go the way I want, I'll make a lot of things my business."

"I don't know what you're talking about."

"Sometimes I think you've cast a spell. Other times I wonder if it's something in the water in Vancouver. Whatever, and despite everything that's happened, I still want you."

Her heart kicked into high gear. She stared at him, her thoughts tumbling. "Want me?" Visions of their night at the island filled her mind. She'd thought she'd never see him again, and he talked of wanting her. Had she entered an alternate universe?

"I want to see you, spend time with you. Hold you. Make love to you. How many ways do you want it spelled out?"

She stared at him, totally at a loss. It was the last thing she expected to hear.

"I'm twenty-eight," she blurted out.

"So, I'm thirty-four. Is that too old for you?"

She shook her head quickly. "No, but I thought you didn't date women over twenty-five."

He frowned. "Where did you get that idea?"

"Mr. Twenty-five/Fifty."

"What does that mean? I heard you say that to the Taylors earlier."

Karla rose and stepped around the chair, putting it between them, holding on for support. "Before I even met you, your reputation preceded you. A man who didn't hire women to work for him that were under fifty and didn't date anyone over twenty-five.''

He stared at her for a long moment. "That's what all this has been about? Some damn-fool notion that I wouldn't hire a woman under fifty?"

She nodded. "I wanted the job. If you didn't hire younger women, I didn't have a chance. So I aged myself a bit. But if you'd look at the application sheet, you'd see I listed my age accurately.''

"I never saw it.''

She kept silent. No use implicating Pat if she didn't need to.

"You don't look twenty-eight, either.''

"I figured you thought I was younger—or you wouldn't have asked me out. That night at the theater I thought you recognized me.''

"You kept looking over at me, I thought it was a pickup.''

Karla almost smiled. "I thought you were picking me up.''

"I did." There was satisfaction in his tone.

"I'm good at my job.''

He nodded once. "I've missed the no-problem response to every request. Even Sarah in Toronto gets flustered, and she's worked for me for years.''

"She's over fifty, I bet.''

"Yes, as a matter of fact, but I inherited her when I took over the firm. Who was this authority who told you about that dumb rule?''

She flushed a little. "Actually I heard a group of secretaries talking at lunch one day.''

"Based on gossip, you came up with this elaborate scheme?"

"It worked."

"Did you plan to retire in fifteen years when I thought you were sixty-five?"

"I planned on telling you everything once I thought you were convinced at how indispensable I was. Actually, my timetable was once the Taylors signed. I thought you'd be in a more receptive mood then."

"And what did you expect my reaction to be?"

She shrugged. "I don't know, angry at first, but unable to let me go. Convinced I was the best for the job."

She gazed at him, wishing they were back on the island, or in the office. Wishing Alice Sawyer hadn't changed her world.

"I'm convinced," he said slowly, his eyes hot with desire. "And unable to let you go."

Hope flared. "I have my job back?"

He shook his head. "I'll find another executive assistant. There were one or two others I interviewed that were on the short list."

"Then I'm not indispensable." Her heart sank. Where was this conversation going?

"Come here, Karla," he said.

She looked at him suspiciously, then slowly came around the chair and walked over to him. Tilting her head back to look into his eyes, she wondered at the intensity of emotions displayed.

"I want you," he said again. "And I suspect you want me. Am I wrong?"

She licked suddenly dry lips.

He slowly lifted his hand to brush her cheek, to sweep back her hair, tangling his fingers in the silky tresses.

When he lowered his head to kiss her, she was ready, eager even for the touch of his mouth against hers, for the tidal wave of heat that swept through her. With a soft inchoate sound, she threw her arms around him and held on. He pulled her tightly against his strength and deepened the kiss.

Was it even sweeter that before, for having gone through the fear of never seeing him again? Was it more sensuous because she knew where such kisses could lead? Was it more loving because she loved him so much her heart felt as if it would burst?

He ended the kiss and looked at her. "I'm glad that's settled. Are you going to invite me to supper?"

"What's settled?" she asked, her heart racing, every nerve in her body tingling in reaction to his kiss. She was wrapped in a warm glow of love and desire and having a bit of trouble concentrating. She wished he'd kiss her again.

"We'll continue seeing each other," he said.

She disengaged herself, feeling like a pail of cold water had been thrown at her. "What do you mean continue to see each other? What about my job? I don't think anything's been settled."

"That kiss said a lot."

"What exactly did it say?" she asked, growing more wary.

"That you want me as much as I want you."

"I want a lot of things, that doesn't mean life is settled and planned out. I want that executive assistant's job. I was good at it, you have to admit that."

"We'll plan to see each other as much as our other commitments allow. But the job's out. I don't mix social and business."

"So we see each other—when?" she asked, feeling chilled by the vision his comment evoked. Where was she going to fall on his priority list? After everything else had been seen to?

"As whenever we want."

"For how long?"

"For as long as we want."

"What if I want forever," she said daringly.

Instantly his expression changed. "I don't do forever."

"Why not?"

"I've explained that. You told me you weren't in the running for the matrimonial stakes. Another lie?"

When Mr. Right comes along, you'll know, Pat had said. Karla was certain she knew. But it didn't appear Mr. Right knew. Or maybe for him, she was not the right one. The thought was depressing.

"Things change," she said slowly.

"Some things don't," he returned.

"For a man who is used to taking risks in business, and even in life with those wilderness treks, you sure are running scared in the personal aspects."

"I'm not going to listen to your pop psychological assessment of my life because I'm not changing it to suit you. We have a lot going for us, could have a lot of fun together. But not forever."

"Impasse," she said, amazed at the calmness of her tone. She wanted to rant and rave and *demand* he love her as much as she loved him. But she knew it wouldn't change anything. Now her only hope was that she could carry this off with a bit of pride.

"Dammit, Karla. I'm not getting married. I thought I made that perfectly clear at the beginning."

"Perfectly," she said, walking over to the sofa and picking up his jacket. She hugged it for a second, breathing in his special scent. She was going to miss him so much. Turning, she held it out.

"You need to go, Matt. Thanks for letting me explain why I pretended I was older. I wish things had worked out differently. I really liked working for you and being with you."

"I'm not leaving."

"Yes. I need for you to leave. I don't want a fling, a casual affair that ends with me heartbroken and eaten up with regrets. Better to part now while we can be friends of a sort."

He strode angrily across the room, and took the jacket. "I have never looked on you as a *friend*," he almost snarled.

"Maybe that's part of the problem. I would have been your best friend as well as lover, and more. If you had given us a chance."

"We can still spend time together."

Did he sound almost desperate? Or was it just wishful thinking on her part?

She shook her head. "I need to make a clean break. Goodbye, Matt. I wish for you all the best life has to offer."

She held her head high, hoping the tears wouldn't fall until after he left. Her throat ached. What kind of gesture would it be if she fell apart and began sobbing?

She opened the door and tried to smile. Her lips trembled and wouldn't cooperate. So be it.

"Karla."

She shook her head, refusing to meet his eyes.

He walked out and hesitated in the hallway. Gently, Karla closed the door. The tears spilled over, tracing down her cheeks. She leaned her head against the cool wooden door, the longing so intense she thought she'd scream with the pain.

Her heart was breaking, she could feel it. How could she have fallen for the man? She knew he was hard and remote—unreceptive to even the thought of a relationship. Blithely she thought she could match his attitude.

But she couldn't. She loved him, wanted to be with him, share her life. And bits and pieces weren't enough. She refused to settle for less than his love and commitment. A lifetime commitment.

The heart doesn't necessarily choose wisely, it just chooses. And it was up to her to pick up the pieces and move on.

She went to bathe her eyes in cool water. Listlessly, she went to heat water for tea. She wasn't hungry, but maybe the tea would soothe. The universal remedy, her mother always said. Even for heartbreak?

The knock startled her. Who was it this time? she wondered. A neighbor? Maybe she wouldn't answer it. No use trying to explain red eyes to a neighbor.

It sounded again, more forcefully.

"Okay, I'm coming," she mumbled, going to the door. Opening it, she was startled to see Matt. His jacket was slung over one shoulder, hooked on his index finger. His tie loosened.

"Matt! I thought you left. What are you doing here?"

He pushed his way into the apartment and reached around her to close the door.

"I got as far as the elevator."

"You've been in the hallway all this time? You left more than ten minutes ago." She didn't get it. What had he been doing for all that time?

He brushed his fingertips along the top of her cheeks. "I never wanted to make you cry," he said softly.

"I'm fine," she said quickly, stepping back. His touch sent pure delight skittering through her. She wasn't sure she could handle the roller coaster of emotions.

His hand encircled the nape of her neck, feeling warm and sensuous. His eyes gazed into hers.

"Well, I'm glad one of us is, then. I'm not."

"What do you mean?"

"You were right."

"About what?" Was she hearing correctly?

"About us. I don't want a casual affair." He took a deep breath. "I want a best friend. I've never had one. And I want a lover who delights me in bed like no one else ever has. A woman who is loyal even when she has no reason to be. A woman who will give a man a second chance. And maybe even a third if he needs it. I want you, Karla."

"I don't get it."

"I'm not sure I do, either. But this last week has been hell. I had a crisis in Toronto, that mostly I wanted to say to hell with since I had more trouble with a certain executive assistant who'd been playing me along. I couldn't believe it. I never in a million years would have guessed your reason. I spent more time envisioning hearing your explanation than dealing with the problem in Toronto. I thought of industrial espionage, of revenge, or just plain craziness.''

''Which maybe it was. I mean, pretending to be fifty just to get a job?''

''A job which you do effortlessly, competently, and enthusiastically. I've never worked with an assistant like you before. You're the best I ever hired.''

She blinked. She wasn't hearing right. Had his touch short-circuited her senses so she imagined things?

''Even if I'm only twenty-eight?''

''I never voiced that rule.'' He looked thoughtful. ''But if people are so concerned with things like that, I can see how the rumor got started—except for the printing firm, all my secretaries have been older women. But in almost every case, they were already working for the company when I bought into it.''

''And the women you date?''

''Younger women are not as interested in settling down. I didn't have a rule about it. But maybe I did have a tendency to date young. The question is now, will you marry me?''

''Marry you?'' Karla's breath whooshed out. She stared at him. *''Marry you?''*

''Say yes.''

''What happened to you were never getting married? To the belief all women were after your bank account?'' Her heart pounded so hard she could hardly hear over the rushing of the blood through her veins. She drew in a ragged breath, her eyes never leaving his. Was he making a joke? *Was it possible he was serious?*

Amusement showed in his eyes. "If you want my bank account, you can have it. But I go with it."

Exasperated she glared at him. "I don't want your bank account."

"But you want me?"

She was imagining things. For a second she thought she glimpsed vulnerability in his eyes when he asked if she wanted him. It couldn't be, not her strong, risk-taking, intrepid Matt Gramling.

Slowly she realized it wasn't imagination. He was uncertain of her response.

As if there were any doubt.

She threw her arms around his neck. "Yes, I want you. I love you, Matt Gramling. I didn't mean to fall in love, but you are irresistible."

His arms tightened around her. She felt as if she'd come home.

"I don't think so, but if you want to think that, hold the thought as long as possible."

He kissed her. Molding her body to his, she could feel the ragged beat of his heart pounding against her. His lips moved persuasively, his tongue dancing with hers, bringing new heights of awareness and desire. Karla floated on a balmy sea of sensation, happiness filling her.

The kaleidoscope of colors behind her lids soared and sparkled. Her breath was gone, but who needed to breathe? She had Matt. Or he had her, it was hard to tell where one left off and the other began he had her wrapped so tightly against him.

Karla didn't have a complaint left in her. Questions, yes, but no complaints.

It was some time before he pulled back enough to gaze

into her eyes. Slowly she opened them and gazed into his.

"Tell me you love me, too," she said. "It's customary, you know."

"I do, Karla Jeannette Jones. I felt as if a part of me had been amputated this last week."

"Next time, give a person a chance to explain. Though as angry as you seemed, I'm not sure you would have listened last Monday. I've felt guilty for weeks, and then when I could explain you wouldn't even let me!"

"I was afraid I was falling for you, fighting it every step of the way," he said slowly. "Then to find out you'd been pretending something that wasn't real, it hit me as hard as Celine's betrayal. I was blindsided. I never expected such a thing. And I could only think of getting away, from you, from the situation." He shook his head. "I never knew I was a coward before."

"You're not! Lisa said you spent all last week in Toronto."

"Good excuse to convince myself I was dealing with business, rather than running away."

"I'm sorry," she said, kissing his chin. Her eyes were sincere. "I planned to tell you as soon as the Taylors signed, honestly. I wouldn't have done it except I wanted the job so much."

"And dating?"

"That I couldn't resist, not after I realized at the theater that you didn't recognize me. You're too potent to refuse."

She gazed at him with all the love shining in her eyes. "So how did we go from you'll never let me come back to work at Kinsinger to a proposal in less than a half hour?'' she asked, snuggling closer, delighting in the feeling of intimacy that wrapped them together.

''I was angry when you kicked me out.''

''No, duh!''

''Don't interrupt. While I waited for the elevator, what you said about risk struck me. Then it opened and was empty. For a second, I saw my life like that. I have no one at home waiting for me at the end of the day. No one to share successes with. No one to completely be myself with. And I saw that empty life down the years. I'm thirty-four. If I want a family to leave the businesses to, or even just a partner to share life with, I need to do something about it.''

''So I'm an old-life alternative.'' She couldn't have imagined a half hour ago she'd ever be teasing him.

He squeezed her. ''I said, no interruptions.''

She tried to look suitably contrite, but she knew the happiness that filled her spilled over.

''So I asked myself how I was going to feel never seeing you again. That put it all into perspective. I'd already had one week without you. I didn't want another, much less a lifetime. If I stopped fighting my age-old beliefs, I suddenly realized you are the perfect woman for me. Look how you took to the island. Look how you took to the job—we could discuss ideas and strategy and you had as many good ideas as I did. Those morning planning sessions became the highlight of my day. I just didn't realize why at the time.''

''Gee, you make it sound so romantic. Morning planning sessions?''

''We'll get to the romantic part in a minute. I'm explaining how I came to my senses.''

"And doing a wonderful job, darling. I love you, Matt."

He looked into her eyes, seeing the warmth and love shining so true. That was all that counted.

"I love you, Karla."

"Partners forever?"

"Forever," he affirmed. He hesitated. "So I don't have to explain any more? You'll marry me?"

"Yes. I'll marry you." She reached up to kiss him long and deeply. Explanations could wait. Or be ignored. The important thing was the end result—a lifetime of happiness for them both.

"I make a great executive assistant, too," she said sometime later, safely wrapped in his arms as they sat side by side on the sofa.

"No! Definitely not. I don't allow family members to work together in my companies. It's not good for business."

"Trust me, Matt, we'll make it work beautifully. No problem."

He did trust her. She held his heart, happiness and hope for the future in her hands. He had been taking risks for years—but this was a sure thing. No problem.

Strong and silent...
Powerful and passionate...
Tough and tender...

Who can resist the rugged loners of the Outback?
As tough and untamed as the land they rule, they
burn as hot as the Australian sun once they meet
the woman they've been waiting for!

Feel the Outback heat throughout 2002 when
these fabulous authors

Margaret Way
Barbara Hannay
Jessica Hart

bring you:

Men who turn your whole world upside down!

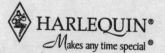

Makes any time special ®

Visit us at www.eHarlequin.com

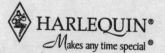HRTA

If you enjoyed what you just read,
then we've got an offer you can't resist!

Take 2 bestselling
love stories FREE!

Plus get a FREE surprise gift!